Marlowe Kana - Volume 3 (Chapters 19-30)

A Word On Sharing:

Please share this book with anyone you see fit.

If you received this book from a friend and liked it, all I ask is that you buy the future volumes and share them with your friends.The individual dollars and pennies don't matter to me nearly as much as being able to write for you. Your financial support is appreciated, but word of mouth is worth 100 times that -- so spread the word, share this book, and keep reading!

Thank you for your support!

Table of Contents

Acknowledgements

Credits
About Joe Peacock
Other books by Joe Peacock
Connect with Joe Peacock

Acknowledgements

Without Beth Watson, Meghan Hetrick, Rowena Yow, Joseph Rhodes, Jason Covert and Casey Edwards, this book would not exist.

For Beth.

19. Lights! Cameras! ACTION!

They had barely made it to the end of the street before Marlowe was ready to stab her own eardrums out. Or stab everyone in the car. Anything to find some peace. As it was, the only weapons she had available to her were the two metal cuffs still fastened around her wrists. She pondered bludgeoning everyone in the car with them, but suspected it would be too much work. She thought wistfully about bashing her own head in. *If I died now, would Imagen let my father go on a technicality? Probably not, ratings for his execution would be too high and far too tempting...*

You're the fucking noob, you NOOB!" Nines hollered at Jen from the back seat.

"The noob who saved your ass!" Jen retorted, red-faced, as she twisted around from the front passenger seat.

"Noob! Hahaha!" Poet cackled as he braked for a stop sign at the end of the road. "That word's funny!"

Marlowe lifted her head slightly from the window she was leaning against, and then let it fall back to the glass with a solid *thunk*.

Nines kicked the back of Jen's seat. "I only had one hand free!" she yelled. "He taped me up and was going to kill me!"

1

Jen rolled her eyes. "Nines, why can't you just admit you needed our help?"

"Uhhh, because I didn't?" Nines replied, rolling her eyes. "And that's not my name. Quit calling me that."

Jen closed her eyes and gritted her teeth. Exasperation poured from her nostrils. "Marlowe," Jen snapped, turning to face her sister. "Do we really need this little brat?"

"Yes," Marlowe said without opening her eyes.

"See??" Nines was triumphant. "You *need* me! But *I* don't need *you*!" Her head bobbed side to side in time with the words she lobbed at Jen.

Marlowe's eyes shot open. She jerked herself upright so quickly the van rattled. "ENOUGH!" She thundered.

Everyone fell silent.

"Jen, you're an adult," Marlowe stated. "Stop acting like a child."

Jen's mouth gaped open. "Me? But *she*--"

"See?" Marlowe said, "That right there. Stop that."

Jen glared at Marlowe, incredulous with disbelief. She turned in her seat and folded her arms over her chest, staring out the window sullenly.

"*Now* who's the brat?" Nines sneered mockingly.

"Nines?" Marlowe whispered as she whipped around to face her. "SHUT. UP."

Nines glared at Marlowe with furrowed brows. She huffed, crossed her own arms over her chest, and stared out the back passenger window as defiantly as Jen.

Marlowe sighed. "We haven't even made it out of the neighborhood yet and you two are ready to kill each other. Which, by the way, I am totally in favor of, if it shuts you both up. But can we wait to do it after, you know, the small task of getting Nine's footage off her servers and freeing our father from prison? Please?"

There was no reply, save from a snicker from Poet in the driver's seat.

"I'll take that as a yes from both of you," Marlowe said. "Poet…why are we stopped?"

"You were talking," he replied through his stifled laughter. "And plus, there's a stop sign…"

"Fucking *drive*, man!" Marlowe said, slapping the headrest of his seat. "We're on the clock!"

Poet hit the accelerator. MagLev engines hummed as the maintenance truck borrowed from the EV plant surged forward. They had hardly passed the welcome sign at the front of the Maple Lanes Subdivision when Nines suddenly sat up in shock.

"SHIT!" she exclaimed, breaking her icy facade. "My countermeasures!"

"What about them?" Marlowe asked.

"I need to go back! I need to wipe everything!"

"Oh my god, you don't have a kill switch?" Jen asked disdainfully, referring to the default safety trigger that required input from the owner at regular, predetermined intervals. If the owner wasn't able to provide that input, the system would self-destruct, assuming that the owner was dead or captured.

"SUCH a fucking noob!" Jen chortled.

Poet snorted. "Noob!"

"Of course I have a killswitch, you bitch!" Nines snapped at Jen. "It's just…you know…not set up yet!"

Jen cackled, stomping her feet on the floorboard of the truck and slapping her legs in glee.

"Shut UP!" Nines barked.

"Can you trigger the self-destruct remotely?" Marlowe interjected.

"Well, yeah," Nines answered, "But how? I'm not augmented, and we left before I could grab my stuff. No one besides your dumb sister is connected, and I'm not trusting her with anything of mine--"

"Here, will this work?" Marlowe asked, tossing to Nines the handheld Pod that the Judge had given her to replace the Pod she'd cut out of her own skull while in prison.

Nines studied the device for a second. "This thing's old," she said as she swiped the screen, tapped it a few times, and inputted some text. She nodded her head. "Yeah, this will work," she said, tapping away on the screen.

"Okay," Marlowe said. "The unlock key is--WHOA!"

Before Marlowe could complete the sentence, a massive flash of light erupted in the pre-dawn sky in the distance, followed by a monstrous *THOOOOOM*! Poet slammed the brakes and the MagLev truck skidded to a halt in the middle of the snowy road. Marlowe, Jen, Nines, and Poet all turned to look out the window. A black plume of smoke billowed orange and red over the spot where Nines' house used to be.

"JESUS!" Jen yelled. "Overkill much?!?"

"I, uh…wanted to be sure," Nines stammered.

"How much freaking explosive did you use?!" Jen asked.

"Uhh…all of it?" Nines answered ruefully.

"Oh my god!" Jen cackled as Nines shrunk back in her seat, pouting.

"Poet, GO!" Marlowe commanded. Poet slammed the throttle stick forward and the truck hummed forward. "Jen? Alerts?"

"Nothing yet," Jen answered, her eyes glowing from the heads-up display in her contacts.

"Well, keep watch. That explosion is definitely going to bring MilSec running."

"You mean the Army," Jen said, her eyes glowing as she scanned the Feeds, catching up on headlines while looking for alerts about the explosion.

"The what?" Marlowe and Poet asked simultaneously.

"President Cook nationalized MilSec," Jen said as she flicked the air. "Happened a few minutes ago. It's now the United American State Army."

"Well, that's fucking stupid," Marlowe said. "Why the hell would he do that?"

"Looks like Cook is taking a stand against Imagen," Jen replied. "Hey, maybe that means MilSec doesn't care about us anymore!"

"Doubtful," Marlowe answered.

"Jesus," Jen said, flicking her finger upward as she scanned story after story. "I've never seen the Feeds so active in my life! It's not even dawn and there's over twenty million people watching. They're still discussing dad and how he supposedly committed treason, and of course you're the number-one topic on just about every top-ten list. Footage from Hax's little camera is being leaked and replayed almost everywhere. You don't even *want* to know what Amanda's been saying about you."

"You're right. I don't," Marlowe said, closing her eyes and resting her head against the window. "In fact, I don't want to hear anything at all right now. I need a nap. Poet, how long until we get back to the EV plant?"

"Thirty minutes or so," he answered.

"Good," Marlowe replied, laying her head against the window and closing her eyes. "Don't wake me for any reason."

A few seconds of silence was all it took for the dull hum of the MagLev engines to gently mirror the thrum of Marlowe's heartbeat. She took a deep breath in through her nostrils, thankful for even the small amount of peace.

"Uh…Marlowe," Poet said quietly.

Marlowe studiously ignored him. She shifted in her seat slightly and adjusted the angle of her neck to prevent the crick she could feel forming. Her back slid slightly down the vinyl seat.

"Marlowe!" Jen barked.

"WHAT" Marlowe roared, her eyes still rebelliously shut.

"Look!"

Marlowe didn't want to look. And yet, she didn't need to. She'd been on enough airborne missions in her career to instinctively know the sound of a Jumper engine, and she suspected she had heard one approaching before she'd even closed her eyes. She gritted her teeth in frustration. She heard Nines gasp and Jen yelp in fear.

Suddenly, Poet shouted, "Hold on!" The aluminum throttle shaft clacked against the metal console as he slammed it forward. The MagLev bellowed and Marlowe felt her body jerk as the truck lurched forward.

She sighed heavily as the darkness behind her eyelids gave way to a red-orange glow. With a deep sigh, she opened her eyes. A focused spotlight shone through the windows of the truck. A United American State Army Jumper was strafing the sky above them, joined by another on the left, and a third behind them.

"Stop the vehicle!" a voice over a loudspeaker ordered.

"Way to go, Nines!" Jen yelled.

"This isn't *my* fault!" Nines retorted.

"They were already on the way," Marlowe said. "Had to be. Poet, find a tunnel!"

"This is the burbs!" Poet said in exasperation as they barrelled down the road.

"Then drive into the forest!" Marlowe ordered.

"What?!" Poet said. "In *this* huge thing? No!"

"You want us to get caught?"

"You want to drive?!" Poet yelled over his shoulder.

"OH, SHIT!" Jen yelled.

Poet whipped his head forward to see far off in the distance flashing blue lights and the silhouette of dozens of troops arrayed in a firing line across the road in front of them.

"Speed up!" Marlowe ordered. "Go through them!"

"Wanna get out and push?!?" Poet snapped back. "We're at max!"

The truck barreled toward the garrison as the three Jumpers matched pace with them.

"Stop! NOW!" The voice on the loudspeaker commanded.

"Don't stop!" Marlowe ordered.

Spotlight drones hovering over the garrison activated in the distance, illuminating the full complement of force that had been sent to deal with Marlowe and her accomplices. Two rows of mobile barricades shielded nearly a hundred soldiers, half kneeling, half standing, all with rifles trained on the truck. Behind them were more soldiers, ducking behind hovering service cars with the new United American State Army logo emblazoned on the digital paint panels. Three massive troop transport trucks hunkered behind the cars.

Two men in powered ExoArmor marched through the gaps in the barricades. They took up stations in front of the riflemen and their barricades, preparing to stop the truck from breaching the roadblock. Mechanized weapons platforms unfolded from their backs and arced over their shoulders, each sporting a GI-9 .50 antipersonnel cannon on their left shoulders, and a BuzzyBee mini-missile swarm launcher on their right. One soldier pounded his oversized robotic fist into his oversized robotic palm. The other extended his arm, encased in a gigantic robotic appendage, and flicked the joystick control in his hand. The palm of the ExoArmor opened, turned upside down, and waved the truck forward, practically begging for them to get through.

"...Okay, on second thought, stop." Marlowe said grimly as the truck got to within two hundred yards of the battalion.

"What!?" Poet, Jen, and Nines all gasped at once.

"We'll never break through all that! Not at this speed!" Marlowe exclaimed. "And even if we could, that Jumper in front of us is seconds away from stuffing a strut through our windshield and reversing its engines! Brakes! NOW!"

Poet gritted his teeth as the garrison in the distance came closer and closer. He pulled the throttle lever back to full stop. The truck lurched and halted with a little over a football field's distance between them and the troops. The three Jumpers in pursuit hovered in place with spotlights trained on the truck, joined shortly by a fourth which took up a position directly in front.

"Hands out of the windows! NOW!" The voice over the loudspeaker commanded.

"Ah shit..." Jen muttered.

"Yeah, we're fucked," Poet added.

Marlowe sighed. "Nines," she said quickly as she reached down and grabbed the go-bag at her feet. "Climb in the front seat next to Jen, and get low–"

"–no *way*!" Nines sneered.

Marlowe's head shot up and her eyes locked with Nines'. The look on Marlowe's face promptly convinced Nines to comply. She clambered between the two front seats and nestled herself into the passenger seat with Jen, who slid over as far as she could toward the door.

"Find that footage right now," Marlowe ordered. "Jen, help however you can. Poet, when I give the signal, you go full reverse, then haul ass someplace safe. If you have to go through a Jumper, do it, but they'll be focused on me."

"Wait, what's the signal?" he asked.

"You'll know it when you see it," Marlowe answered as she placed an AMP inhaler between her lips. She depressed the button and inhaled deeply, taking another full dose of the quadruple-strength drugs Jen had provided. She shivered.

"Hands out the window or we open fire!" The loudspeaker barked.

"Do it," Marlowe ordered to Jen and Poet. "Just you two. Nines, stay low."

Poet reached forward to the console and pushed two buttons, lowering the driver and passenger-side windows. Slowly, Jen and Poet both stuck their hands out of the window.

Marlowe rolled down her window and placed both of her hands out as well.

"Marlowe Kana!" The loudspeaker voice barked. "Out of the car – just you. No one else!"

Marlowe looked at her sister and flashed a crooked smile. "Get our dad out, whatever it takes," she said.

"Marlowe," Jen whispered, voice quivering with fear. "What are you going to do?"

"Turn myself in," she answered as she pulled the lever on the rear passenger door. It swung open. Slowly, Marlowe stepped out.

"Close the door behind you!" The loudspeaker voice commanded. Marlowe gently closed the door, bringing it just shy of latching.

"Hands up!"

Marlowe complied.

Ropes spilled from either side of the Jumper behind the truck. Heads peeked out, ensuring the area was safe. Four United American State soldiers rappelled out of the Jumper, two from each side, while one remained in a sniper's position up in the hovering transport, rifle trained on Marlowe. The soldiers touched down and immediately moved into formation, approaching Marlowe with extreme caution.

"Hands on the vehicle!" The lead soldier ordered as the team slowly approached. "Do it!"

Marlowe, hands raised over her head, turned and faced the door. She slowly lowered her right hand, resting it on the top of the door and slyly wrapped her fingers around the top of the frame. As she lowered her left hand, she gently pulled the door slightly open. As her left hand touched the door, she slid it quickly along the open edge and yanked the door open, spinning herself behind it for cover. With a grunt, she pressed her body into the door, folding it against the frame until the hinges sheared and tore loose with a grinding *SHRIEK*! Marlowe fixed her hands around the armrest and the door like a shield. She pressed forward and began sprinting toward the soldiers.

"FIRE!" The lead soldier screamed.

Fingers pulled triggers. The sound of a dozen empty trigger clicks echoed all around, followed by another dozen. None of the trademark whizzing of Imagen railgun magnets spooling could be heard; no reports echoed as slugs should have left the muzzle of a barrel. The only thing they could hear was the crunching of Marlowe's footsteps through the snow.

"Oh, shit," the lead soldier whispered. He watched down the sights of his defunct rifle as Marlowe ducked her head behind the door, her eyes disappearing beneath the window. She lunged forward, ramming full-force into the the soldiers, sending each one flying like bowling pins in a perfect strike. Instinctively, Marlowe raised the door directly over her head to shield from the sniper's shot, which to her amazement, never came.

She looked up through the window of the door to see a confused sniper smashing her palm into the receiver of her malfunctioning weapon. Not one to question good fortune on the battlefield, Marlowe reared back and flung the door like a discus toward the Jumper. The sniper looked up from her broken rifle in time to see the car door collide with the right wing, tearing through the MagLev engine mounted underneath. A shower of sparks and spindles of lightning erupted from the engine, electrocuting the sniper and sending her crashing down on top of two soldiers who were just getting to their feet.

The Jumper lurched as the pilot attempted to adjust for the loss of the engine. He overcorrected, sending the

Jumper yawing violently over in mid-air. Marlowe crouched, then leapt into a backwards somersault, narrowly escaping the Jumper as its remaining MagLev engine slammed into the ground less than a meter from where she had been standing. The other soldiers were immediately crushed in the wreckage.

Without losing a moment, Marlowe ran back to the wreckage, grabbing a soldier's useless rifle along the way. She shoved the butt end of the weapon into the wobbling air intake spindle of the remaining engine of the Jumper, bringing it to an abrupt halt. She seized the blades of the turbine and yanked back as hard as she could, pulling it clean off the spindle. Ignoring the searing heat, she turned and flung the fan like a frisbee. It whipped through the air past the EV plant truck and sailed into the first of the two ExoArmored soldiers who were sprinting her way full speed.

The rotor struck the facemask of the left-hand soldier's helmet and tore through it like a sawblade, sending a showering mist of blood into the air and his body tumbling head-over-heels backward. The other soldier turned to look in frank horror. As he glanced swiftly back toward the truck, he was more horrified to see how quickly Marlowe had suddenly covered the distance between them.

He had no time to react as Marlowe left her feet and somersaulted over him. She grabbed the impact bars extending up and over the shoulders of the soldier's ExoArmor, and as she brought herself around to land, pulled the soldier off his feet and over her head. With every ounce of power in her body, she flung him forward and heaved the metal-clad body thirty yards through the air before he crashed down onto the snow-covered roadway. His arms and legs flailed as he skidded the rest of the distance toward the garrison, scraping to a stop just as his head gently tapped the barricade.

The soldier sat up groggily, thankful to somehow be alive. But before he could complete the thought, he felt Marlowe's left foot land on the frontispiece of his ExoArmor, and her right foot stomp directly on top of his helmet. Marlowe launched off of his helmet and over the barricades, where she landed directly in the center of a crush of soldiers all rushing forward in the mad hope of being the one to collar Marlowe Kana.

"Goddammit, FIRE!" A captain bellowed over the loudspeaker behind layers of barricades, soldiers, trucks, and tanks as Marlowe tore into the soldiers. The empty clicks of triggers sang like crickets all around. Marlowe grabbed a rifle from one of the circle of soldiers around her, drew back, and and clubbed its former owner on the back of the skull. He doubled over. She leapt up, stepped on his head, and launched herself off his back onto the top of one of the tanks directly behind the line of riflemen. The soldiers, finally convinced their guns were useless, dropped them and swarmed over to the tank where Marlowe stood perched on the end of the barrel. They all stood and watched in awe as she stared down at them.

"This doesn't have to happen," she said to the crowd of mesmerized soldiers. "Let us go and I'll spare your lives."

"Take her DOWN!" The captain screamed over the loudspeaker.

A roar erupted as the soldiers began yelling and climbing up the tank.

"Well, I tried," Marlowe said with a shrug. She sprang from the tip of the tank's gun like a diver, flipped through the air, and came crashing down on top of the group of soldiers, fist on knee. The soldier she landed on spat blood onto the inside of his faceplate as several of his internal organs ruptured.

Marlowe stood and spun with her fist out, clipping a soldier in the helmet with her metal cuff. With another spin, she flung her foot out and nailed another soldier in the sternum with a perfectly placed kick, stopping him in his tracks. She whipped her leg up and around and caught the solder around the neck, then flung him to the ground, snapping his spine. A dozen more soldiers swarmed her, all piling on top of her at once. They grabbed her arms and her legs, attempting to subdue her. She smashed the two soldiers holding her arms together helmet-to-helmet, knocking them out. Two more took their place. She slammed one on the helmet with the cuff around her wrist, and the other she seized by the throat. She began spinning, using the limp soldier's boots as a flail as she cleared a circle around her. Letting go of the sweeper, Marlowe sent him flying head-first through the windshield of one of the troop transports.

A Jumper approached and hovered just over her head. Soldiers leapt from either side of it, landing directly in front of her. She crouched, then sprung directly up, latching onto the strut of the Jumper. The pilot tried shaking her off with frantic, jerky movements. She climbed aboard and seized him by the hair, slamming his face into the console. Grabbing the pilot's joystick and throttle, she shot the Jumper straight up. With a twist of the controls, she pitched the Jumper forward until it was pointed nearly straight down. She leapt out just before it crashed on the tank she was perched on earlier, taking out a dozen soldiers in the fiery explosion.

Marlowe landed, rolled forward, and then made a beeline for the corner of the intersection the garrison was blockading. She was relieved to see that she was right – an antique stop sign was still sitting there. Normally, she despised the kitschy callbacks to the so-called simpler times before the war, but this time, she was thankful for the nostalgia. She seized the post and plucked it from the ground, wielding the giant octagonal sign like Death's scythe.

"Goddammit!" The captain barked over the loudspeaker. "Killjoys! Now!"

"Sir!" One of the soldiers could still be heard over the live mic. "Didn't you read the brief? They don't–"

"--Don't question me, private!" the captain demanded. "Do it!"

Drones flew from the back of one of the United American State tanks and swarmed around Marlowe. High-voltage electrical shocks lanced from the drones' terminals, attempting to tase her into submission.

Marlowe's body flexed. Power surged through her. The pain was incredible, but did nothing to incapacitate her. Instead, a bellow erupted from her lungs as she swung the stop sign like a bat, connecting with the drones and sending them flying. One crashed through the windshield of a garrison truck. Electric shocks danced around the hovering transport, sending it lurching forward in a fury. It crashed into a throng of soldiers rushing toward Marlowe, mowing them down.

Marlowe leapt into the air with the stop sign, both hands clutching it like an axe. With immense fury, she brought it down on one of the soldiers, cleaving him down the middle. She swung the sign in an arc, blood spattering on the other soldiers as it slammed into another, slicing his armor through and leaving his guts spilling onto the road.

"Retreat!" One of the soldiers yelled. The others didn't question. They turned as one and began running away.

"What are you doing!?" The captain screamed. "You have orders! GET her!"

Marlowe turned toward the captain's vehicle. She sprinted forward, the concrete plug at the base of the stop sign in front of her like a jouster's lance. The captain's eyes widened. He ducked just as the post crashed through the driver's-side window of his door.

Marlowe ripped the door off its hinge and sent it, along with the stop sign, flying behind her into two more soldiers she didn't even realize were there. She yanked the captain out of his car by his boot. Clawing desperately at the seats, he emerged from the vehicle, and felt himself being whirled around as Marlowe spun him in a dizzying circle. She released, and the captain flew through the air into a Jumper that was attempting to join the fight. It didn't succeed. Instead, the Jumper merged with the captain's body, and the bloody amalgam crashed into the remaining tank, exploding in a brilliant, blue-orange electrical fireball.

Further chaos erupted as soldiers attempted to escape, while others wrestled with the prospect of imminent death. Several others had delusions of eternal WarFeed glory, imagining that they would be the hero who took down Marlowe. They formed a line and approached Marlowe, who turned to face them. She took a few steps forward and grabbed the stop sign still hanging from the captain's car door. She held the door up with her left arm as a shield, and wielded the stop sign like a mace in her right.

The soldiers froze. There was no entry in the field operations manual about door-and-stop-sign-wielding augmented supersoldiers.

"Run, idiots!" One of the soldiers screamed as he broke rank and began sprinting down the road. Another took out a Pod, turned his back to Marlowe, and snapped a quick selfie – the photo captured the moment the stop sign connected with his helmet. The other soldiers tried to subdue Marlowe, but were cut down as she rammed the door into their heads and sliced them to pieces with her makeshift gladiatorial weapon.

Over ninety soldiers lay dead, burned and sliced and in parts and pieces, as cars and tanks and Jumpers burned around Marlowe. The remaining Jumper landed a few dozen yards away, and boarded the remaining soldiers who were smart enough to flee. Packed to the gills, it began to lift off. Marlowe thought briefly about letting them go.

Nah.

She heaved the door at the Jumper, catching the tail stabilizer and sending it spinning as it lifted up. It tipped and crashed spectacularly, killing everyone inside.

The snow glowed orange and red and blue around Marlowe as fires burned and electrical showers erupted. What soldiers weren't hacked to pieces or burned alive rolled in agony in a litany of broken bones, spines, and spirits. She stood holding the blood-drenched stop sign with her back arched and face toward the sky, heaving from exhaustion. Unclenching her fists, she let the makeshift weapon fall with a muffled thud into the streets, the classic red of the American stop sign blending with the blood-drenched snow. She leaned forward and put her hands on her knees as she gasped for air. She looked up at the truck as it slowly approached. She caught a glimpse of Poet's gaping mouth and Jen's widened eyes. For the first time in months, she smiled in genuine happiness.

"Truck door's still back there," she said through her panting, pointing toward the smoldering wreckage of the first Jumper she felled. "I don't think it's gonna go back on, though."

"Probably not," Poet said numbly from the window.

"You okay?" Jen asked across Poet from the passenger seat.

"Never better," Marlowe replied. "Why are you still here?"

"You cut off our escape route," Poet answered, pointing to the wreckage. "Besides, Nines wanted to get footage of–"

"–OH MY GOD, THAT WAS EPIC!" Nines screamed as she poked her head up from between Jen and Poet. "Look! I got some great footage!" She held the Pod's screen up for Marlowe to see.

"Delete it," Marlowe commanded briskly as she entered the truck and took a seat in the back.

"Too late!" Nines said as a small *DING!* chirped from the Pod's speaker. "Already up to twenty-thousand views!"

Marlowe sighed. "Jen. Why didn't you stop her?"

"What am I, her nanny? Besides, she won't listen to me."

"Because you're dumb," Nines said.

"You're going to get us killed," Marlowe said.

"I'm going to make us RICH!" Nines answered. "On-the-scene footage of Marlowe Kana destroying over a hundred soldiers? And it's not from a soldier's bodycam? Do you know how *valuable* this is?"

"Not nearly as valuable as the footage that clears my name," Marlowe said, leaning her head back against the headrest. "Why don't you have that yet? And Poet, *why* are we not hauling ass to the EV plant?"

"Orders," Poet responded. "The Judge just radioed. He's inbound."

"Oh, goody," Marlowe replied. "We'll just wait here while he comes to tour the damage. Hopefully the soldiers' guns still don't work when reinforcements arrive. And speaking of that. Anyone know why their rifles malfunctioned?"

"...Orders?" Poet said quizzically. "Maybe they were told not to shoot?"

"Definitely not," Marlowe replied. "They were yanking triggers as hard as they could. Their weapons... somehow they malfunctioned." Marlowe looked at Jen. "Did you..."

Jen shook her head. "Way above my level," she answered as she glanced back at her sister. The two exchanged a look. Together, they both turned to face Nines.

"What?" Nines asked. "You think I hacked their weapons via a stupid handheld Pod connected to PublicNet? Come on...that kind of shit only happens in movies. OOH! Speaking of movies, check out this video I cut together while you were walking back to the truck!"

Nines held the Pod up toward Marlowe. Scenes from various soldiers' body cameras flashed in quick succession, each one showing Marlowe smashing a fist, foot, or dislodged portion of a vehicle into them. Cut after cut of Marlowe's face, fists, and feet flickered on the screen. "I scraped soldier Feeds while they were fighting you. Genius, right?" Another FeedMeter *DING!* sounded.

Marlowe shut her eyes and sighed as she shrunk back into her seat.

Nines looked crestfallen. "I know, you hate your own videos, but come on…I did this in less than a minute! I thought you'd be impressed!"

Marlowe groaned. She closed her eyes and rolled her head toward Nines. Her mouth gaped open and she began snoring.

"She's shutting down," Jen said. "Don't take it personally."

Reading the sadness that fell over Nines' face, Jen softened. "Look, I'm sure she would, if she was able to. She's completely drained. She can run on Battery bars, adrenaline, and AMP for only so long." Jen chuckled as she added, "besides, I thought you didn't like her. At least, that's what you said at your place." She winked and flashed a sarcastic smile at Nines.

Nines' lip quivered. A tear rolled down her cheek. Suddenly, she flushed and her eyes narrowed. "I don't!" Nines shouted at Jen. "I *don't* like her! And I don't like you! *Either* of you! And I don't like this stupid truck. I don't like anything, okay?! Leave me alone!"

Jen looked at Poet, who shrugged. Trying to make peace, she tapped the air a few times and pulled up Nine's video on the MKFan_9999 channel. "Huh…this really is a good video, Nines. Good work."

"Fuck you, noob," Nines said, arms folded over her chest as she stared out the window.

Poet couldn't help but laugh.

A tone sounded in the cabin of the truck. "Go ahead," Poet answered.

"We're inbound," the Judge announced. "Please tell Marlowe not to throw a car door at us."

Poet looked in the rearview mirror to find Marlowe flopped across the back seat, mouth open, snoring.

"That doesn't seem to be a risk," Poet responded.

20. A Day In The Life Of: Marc Winter

Marc couldn't have been any happier in his elected position as Personal Service Professional at the Waffle House on Courtland Street. Sure, human service wasn't often requested by customers, so he spent most of his nights leaned back against the wall with his high-tops on the counter, watching the Feeds. But on the rare occasion that customers requested that they be served by a living, breathing human being, Marc Winter was ready to go.

He'd been at this position for nearly thirty years -- long enough for his hair to go from black, to grey, to gone. His ebon scalp shined almost as brightly as the smile perpetually stamped across his face, which forced the tips of his thick grey moustache to turn up jauntily at the edges. Marc had plenty to smile about. His granddaughter had just been accepted into the Imagen Advanced Training Academy, the exact week his daughter had graduated from the same illustrious institution - the first person in the family to do so, despite her late entry. Neither would have been able to go if not for his years of Superior Grade performance at the Waffle House. Being one of the few living recipients of a pre-MilSec Purple Heart didn't hurt, nor did his impeccable service record for his enlistment during the Second Civil War. But even wartime heroics against the terrorists and separatists weren't enough to guarantee entry to such an exclusive educational track at his social level. And that was why he chose to work. S-Grade in a chosen job was a sure ticket to success.

And he didn't mind the labor. As jobs went, this one was pretty easy, and came with the perk of always being up to date on NewsFeed. But his daddy had raised him right. He never took something for nothing. "Even if every citizen had a right to guaranteed income from Imagen," his father had lectured, "A real man works for his wage. Get up, get out, and get something." Even if that something meant sitting on a stool at a counter endlessly smiling at anyone who came in, hoping in vain that they may actually want you to serve them. No matter what, it sure beat living off the Imagen dole.

And that's why he liked Regina and Reginald Todd and their weird friend Tad. The twins and Tad had been coming into the Waffle House on Courtland and drinking bottomless cups of coffee every weekend for nearly four years. Marc loved those three kids. He knew them to be good kids. Most kids, when they reached the age of thirteen and the curfews and limits on drugs lifted, went crazy for a little while. They'd hit the Subs for booze and pills and got all that wandering out of their system. The Todd twins and Tad, though, just stuck to the classics: sugary syrup on their pecan waffles and good ol' fashioned black caffeine.

The kids sat at the corner table every Saturday and Sunday from midnight until dawn discussing everything and anything from social issues and history to animation. Occasionally, they would bring in a bag full of dice and some paper with grid lines on it and make maps for their GURPS tabletop role-playing game.

This time, however, they were late. Really late. It was nearly five in the morning when they finally came traipsing in, jittery as hell, with their hoods pulled over their heads. It didn't take a genius to see that they'd been up to no good.

They didn't even ask J.A.Q.i to send "Marc the Man" over to get them their coffee. It was fine though, Marc didn't take offense. It was just an oversight. It'd happened before. The kids came in all hot and heavy in discussion about history or politics or art or WarFeed and got distracted. He didn't worry about such slights, because he knew they'd want him to serve them even if they forgot to ask. What *did* have him worried, however, was the fact that he couldn't get any of the three to look up at him when he sauntered up to their table.

"Kids?" Marc asked softly for the third time. "You okay?"

"We're fine," Reggie said, face buried behind his hands. "Coffees."

"Well, okay," Marc said slowly. "Three black coffees coming right - oh wait! Looky here! They're already in front of ya!" He gestured with his tray toward the three steaming mugs he'd placed before them.

Regina looked up from a nest of raven-black hair. Her bright-red face was streaked black with mascara and green with what looked like paint. Her hands were the same shade of green. She looked past her brother who was sitting slumped beside her and managed to lock her ice-blue eyes on Marc. The second she saw the concern in the gentle old man's face, she broke into heart-wrenching sobs.

"Sweetheart!" Marc said in dismay. "What's got you shook? All three y'all look like you saw a ghost!"

"The walls..." Tad said from his side of the table with a shudder. "The walls aren't working! THEY AREN'T WORKING! We almost DIED because the damn WALLS AREN'T WORKING!"

"Cool it!" Reggie barked as he banged the table, startling Tad and causing Regina to plop her face back into the pile of her arms.

"Okay, what the hell is going on?" Marc said. "This ain't you! This ain't none of you!"

Reggie was still refusing to look at Marc. He gestured limply at the screen on the wall across from where they sat.

Marc looked over to see NewsFeed coverage of Marlowe's thorough annihilation of over a hundred United American State Army soldiers. Amanda Stokes was at the helm, viciously condemning the horror Marlowe had just perpetrated and blaming her for starting a "wave of insubordination, depravity, and social violence across Atlanta and across the nation."

"J.A.Q.i, switch on audio to NewsFeed," Marc said aloud. The delightful country twang of Waffle House's background music faded, and the audio from NewsFeed rose.

"Unbelievable is right!" Stokes sneered as her face shrank to a small window in the bottom-left corner of the screen, highlighting the drone footage of Marlowe Kana kicking the helmet off of one soldier's head and into the groin of another. "This is disgusting! Our soldiers aren't even shooting at her, and she proceeds to treat them like rag dolls! I can't believe we are airing this...this...travesty of justice! Bobby, can we cut this? Can we please stop giving airtime to this felon? "

"No," a voice was heard saying off-screen.

"No? NO!?!" Amanda barked. "This is MY show! Cut it!"

More mumbling from off-camera and then a muffled, "I can't. Order from Imagen is for full-spectrum."

"So this is on *every* Imagen Feed?!?" Amanda said, incredulous. "You know what, Bobby? You're right. This is unbelievable! Absolutely abhorrent!" Amanda slammed her fists on her desk. "I can't DO this anymore!" She shrieked. "MK is a traitor, a felon, a violent criminal... just *look* at this footage! She just set one of our soldiers on fire! That we nurture the celebrity status she so deeply craves, even

after being found guilty of betraying our country...
betraying us...is downright disgusting. It's bad enough that
she's considered news, but to be on every network,
smashing up MilSec vehicles and soldiers--"

"--Army," Bobby interrupted from off-camera.

Amanda's face contorted. "Even worse!" she snarled.
"United American State Army isn't even an hour into its
existence and it's being torn apart by this criminal!"

Marc looked grimly away from the screen. "You kids
are upset about MK?" He asked. "I know, I'm upset, too.I
always loved watching her Feeds. You know, she came in
here once? She sat right over--"

"--No," Reggie interrupted, finally looking up at Marc.
"*That*." He pointed back at the screen.

Marc turned to see NewsFeed correspondent Tom
Wallace standing in front of the downtown Atlanta precinct
of the newly christened United American State Army. He
was gesturing with his non-microphone hand toward a huge
swatch of green paint vivid against a white marble wall. "If
we can zoom out, Mike?" Tom asked his camera drone
operator. "Can you pull it back?"

The camera drone eased back and showed Tom
standing next to a gigantic, six-foot high exclamation point.
The drone pulled back further, as did the mounted spotlight.
The light faded, and the screen went black.

"Just a moment," Tom Wallace said to the audience. "Mike, a few light drones?"

A moment passed. The screen glared all white as five drones activated their mounted spotlights. The iris of the camera drone adjusted and into view loomed a massive, bright-green graffiti tag that read, "#FREEMARLOWE!"

"HA! THAT'S FANTAS--" Marc quickly caught himself. He leaned into the kids and lowered his voice to a whisper. "That's fantastic! You kids made the NewsFeed with your art!"

"But the walls don't WORK!" Tad shouted. He was shaking uncontrollably. "They don't WORK tonight because of all this craziness with Marlowe, and we almost DIED!"

"He's right!" Regina cried. "They were going to shoot us! I heard the clicking of their triggers. They would have *shot* us! They've never done that before!"

"I don't understand." Marc said. "You guys come in here every night after you tag walls. You've hit that place before! Why did they decide to come after you tonight? And *shooting*?"

"The sanitation drones...the self-cleaning walls..." Reggie said. "They all got all messed up in the switch from Milsec to Army, like the guns."

"The guns? What guns? And what do you mean 'messed up?' What is going on?" Marc asked, watching as NewsFeed switched back to clips of Marlowe's exploits.

"That's what Private Mitchell said," Reggie answered. "He usually just lets us tag, because hey, why not? The scrubbers get the walls before anyone even notices, and he'd rather we get the street cred for being the ones who tag MilSec stuff. But tonight, he...he wasn't..." Reggie broke down in tears.

"Alone," Tad whispered. "He wasn't alone. Entire squad...all of them pissed as hell..."

"They pointed their guns at us!" Regina said tearfully. "They *shot* at us!"

Marc was dumbfounded. He suddenly remembered what it was like just after the war, when he was their age. Being targeted by rampaging, out-of-control separatists for the crime of simply being a young black teenager from the south. He always thought it was so fortunate that these kids were given the means to act out in safe ways - getting a taste of activism with no real risk. And he knew that their tagging had been getting popular, to the point that he had heard of the Todd And Tad Crew even outside of The Waffle House. They got access to targets that other crews didn't have the balls to go after, mostly because they were good kids who did good work.

But to face their own mortality this violently had suddenly put the fear of God in them. They were finally witnessing the true price of freedom -- those who controlled it were without boundary on how to acquire it from you. Even to the point of shooting at a group of teenagers for doing something no one had cared about the day before, simply because it had been decided to suddenly enforce a law that hadn't been in place since the early 2000's.

"J.A.Q.i, private booth," Marc commanded. A bright blue hexagonal matrix danced and rose around the booth where the teenagers sat.

"Listen up now, 'cause I want you to hear me," Marc said in a tone of voice he'd not heard come out of his own mouth in nearly fifty years. "Look up at me. Right now."

It took a while, but eventually, all three teeangers lifted baleful eyes up at Marc.

"Them soldiers is mad. They don't have control right now. They look like fools, with the thumping MK gave them and now your tag not being scrubbed. They're reeling. And they're going to be reacting. Hard."

The kids stared up at this kindly old man who had served them coffee for years as the smile creases in his face disappeared and his eyes narrowed. "Authority don't like it when they see how little they have."

The kids sat up and took deep breaths. "We almost died," Regina finally said in horrified wonder.

"Almost," Marc said with a smile and a wink, his former genial demeanor returning. "You want creamer with that coffee?"

Regina chuckled. Tad cracked a smile. Reggie straightened himself, looked up at Marc, and said, "Marc, you ask me that every night."

"That I do," he said with a grin.

"And we always say no," Reggie continued, an obvious note of relief creeping into his voice.

"That you do," Reggie said. He turned to leave, but then paused. He glanced at the screen on the wall, which was showing dueling, side-by-side panel footage from MK's fight with the troops on the left, and a wide shot of the #FREEMARLOWE! tag that the Todd and Tad Crew had plastered on the precinct wall.

He looked back at Regina and Reginald Todd and their weird friend Tad. "You don't always know it when it happens," Marc said as he turned to leave. "But sometimes, doing what you do changes the world."

"How does some graffiti that can't be washed off change the world?" Tad called after him.

"I don't really know just yet," Marc Winters said over his shoulder. "But I have a feeling it's gonna."

21. Too Many Cooks

The sound of splintering wood was the high note in the chorus of chaos as a colossal, armored Secret Service soldier crashed through the door of the Presidential bedroom. The sudden explosion of noise caused President Cook to jerk violently, shoving deeper in the shard of glass that he was attempting to extract from the sole of his left foot.

"FUCK!" Cook shrieked.

"Perimeter sweep!" The soldier barked. Three other soldiers barged in and began checking the room through the sights of their rifles. "Are you okay, sir?" The first soldier queried as he approached Cook.

"What the fuck does it *look* like?!?" Cook slurred. "No, I'm not okay! I have glass buried in my foot and I'm bleeding and what on earth are you DOING in here!?! And why do you have rifles? They don't even work! Haven't you seen NewsFeed?"

"We heard a commotion, sir," the soldier answered as he stood within a hair's breadth of the President. "We thought your safety was compromised."

"What…get away from me!" The President shouted, drunkenly attempting to shove the soldier aside. Physics being what they were, Cook instead only succeeded in flailing backward toward the bed. He instinctively slammed his feet to the ground to regain balance and the glass embedded in his foot penetrated even deeper.

"Fuck! *Christ*!" Cook shouted. "NOW look what you did!"

"J.A.Q.i, medical team!" The soldier barked.

"No!" Cook countered. "J.A.Q.i, don't send anyone, I'll be fine…"

The Secret Service leader grimly surveyed the wreckage littering Cook's bedroom. Most obvious was the glowing rainbow sputtering behind a spiderweb of glass that was once the wall-sized screen. The distinct red bar of a NewsFeed Breaking News tag could barely be made out in the upper-right corner. Broken pieces of a chair that had held many former Presidents' posteriors as they worked at the Resolute Desk (once the centerpiece in the original Oval Office in Washington D.C. - now a writing desk in the President's bedroom in Indianapolis) lay in splinters and chunks underneath the screen, as did the remnants of several shattered whiskey tumblers. A drink cart sat overturned in the corner of the room, chunks of whiskey-soaked crystal lay in a soggy pool on the carpet. The audio from NewsFeed was staticky and faint as Amanda Stokes recounted once again the highlights of Marlowe Kana's single-handed defeat of over one hundred United American State Army Soldiers -- an event she'd since dubbed "The Massacre At Maple Lane."

This soldier had seen his share of violent wreckage in his various tours over the years…but this was by far the best story he'd never be able to tell anyone.

"Room's clear, sir!" One of the secret service soldiers barked.

"Stand down. Assume guard," the leader ordered. The soldiers lowered their rifles. Two of them assumed posts at the doorway and the third maintained watch over the main window.

"Sir," the leader said as he returned his attention to Cook. "It seems you've been consuming alcohol and that you are bleeding profusely. You need medical attention."

"It seems you didn't get the memo that I am the fucking PRESIDENT of the United American State, and I need you to leave me the FUCK alone!" Cook screamed.

"I must insist, sir," the leader answered. Before Cook could further protest further, two of the staff doctors arrived with a Medi-Drone. They immediately took up positions next to the President.

"Oh, God," Cook said frantically. "I don't need this! I don't need you! Get *out*! Get out NOW -- OUCH!" He slapped his right arm as a needle slid free from his skin. "What the hell did you shoot me with!?!"

"Sobering agent and blood-clotting agent, sir," one of the doctors said calmly as she dropped the needle on the MediDrone's tray without even looking at Cook's direction. A hatch opened atop the Medi-drone as the doctor reached toward it. She grabbed a pair of forceps while the other doctor lifted and held Cook's foot.

Cook tried to struggle, but found he couldn't jerk his leg away from the doctors or even wiggle his toes. "What the...I can't move!"

"There was a nerve agent as well, sir," the doctor holding his foot said. "So we can work."

"That's *assault*!" Cook yelled. "You just assaulted the President!"

The doctor with the forceps extracted the glass shard from the President's foot and placed it on a tray held by the Medi-Drone. She dropped the bloody forceps on the tray next to the glass and grabbed a small bottle with saline and began irrigating the wound.

"Soldier, arrest these people!" Cook ordered. "I want them...I..." Cook stopped mid-sentence. He'd suddenly realized that not only was he completely sober, but that he had clearly been acting like an ass for the better part of the last half hour.

"Clean," the doctor irrigating the wound said to the other holding Cook's foot, who held up a small spray bottle and coated the wound with a liquid suture. The cut closed itself immediately.

Cook watched as the doctor who had extracted the glass pricked him with another needle. A numb rush swept over his body. For a fraction of a second, he could feel every single nerve ending dancing and tingling. Feeling returned to his limbs. His head cleared.

"Wow," the President said as a wave of euphoria washed over him. "Well...good work. I seem to be...better now. Thank you."

"It's our job, sir," the doctor at his feet said as he lowered Cook's leg. He began scanning the President's body and checking vitals while the other doctor held her fingers to Cook's neck.

"Really, I'm okay now," The President demurred. "I just...I really need some sleep."

Just then, a line of cleaning drones wheeled their way into the Presidential bedroom and dutifully began clearing up the mess. One vacuumed up chunks of broken glass; another dragged splintered and cracked (and priceless) antique wood fragments out of the room. Three of the bots began scrubbing the blood from the carpet.

"Out, okay?" The President asked quietly, a headache starting to throb at his temples. "All of you out. This can all be done tomorrow."

"The drones need to clean and the doctors need to be certain you're okay, sir," the leader of the secret service team said over the din of clanking cleaner drones. "Once they've cleared you and the drones have made the room safe, we will be on our way."

A tone sounded throughout the room. "Sir," J.A.Q.i announced, "Chairman Davis for you."

"Fuck him," Cook said quietly. "Hang up."

"Sir, as you know, I'm an Imagen system," J.A.Q.i replied. "He's the Chairman of the Board and has overridden disconnects. I can't."

Cook sighed. He sat up straight and cleared his throat. "Everyone out. Now."

The soldiers didn't move. The doctors continued monitoring his vital signs.

Cook stood. "OUT!" he barked, pointing to the door. "Or you're fired!"

The soldiers and doctors exchanged glances. Reluctantly, they all filed out the door.

"Drones out, too!" Cook commanded. The robots stopped their cleaning and began rolling toward the door. Cook walked over and punted one, nearly breaking his toe in the process. He pushed the door closed, but due to the severe manner in which it had been opened, it didn't quite close all the way.

"Okay, let's get this over with," Cook said aloud. Another tone sounded.

"Stephen!" Davis barked immediately, his words seeming to stab directly into Cook's throbbing skull. "*Tell* me this was part of your plan! Tell me you intended to steal my entire security force only to render them inert, feeding them to that wolf of a woman in front of the entire nation! *Tell* me how our own citizens are now emboldened to graffiti a MilSec station! Tell me how open revolt and a super-powered terrorist contribute to your ridiculous plot to return the United American State to some kind of former glory! Unless that glory, of course, results in a THIRD Civil War, you...you *imbecile*!"

"Engagement, Alan," Cook answered coolly as he returned to his bed. "It's always about engagement. Trust me, it's all part of the plan."

"Oh, there was certainly engagement!" Davis scoffed. "Marlowe Kana just *engaged* several squads of soldiers in front of an audience of forty million people -- to a bloody end! The Subs in Atlanta are still smoldering, and now, our citizens are taking to defacing National property!"

"They've always done that," Cook interjected. "It's art."

"It's embarrassing is what it is!" Davis yelled. "And yes, it's all great footage, if *that* was your goal, but now the entire nation knows that our *guns* don't *work*! Which is also your fault! Yes, sir, the citizens of the United American State will be engaged for *weeks* with this...this..."

"It was a calculated move," Cook interjected, wincing as he rubbed the newly formed scar on his foot.

"You calculated this?!?" Davis yelled. "You hijacked our entire nation's security and military division and didn't update the code on the biometric weapons lockout system on *purpose*?!? It was a calculated move to render over a hundred thousand soldiers both domestic and in the Gaslands absolutely defenseless? That was on PURPOSE?"

"Of course," Cook bluffed. "Everything will be explained in due time–"

"-NOW is the time, Stephen! Explain yourself!"

"Goddammit, Alan!" Cook snapped. "You haven't seen the bigger picture like I have! You'll understand soon enough. For now, I'm exhausted. I need some sleep. Goodnight, Alan." He waved his hand in the air and the call was placed on hold. *He may have the connection locked,* he thought, *but that doesn't mean I have to hear him...*

Cook stewed. He could kick himself for such a minor oversight, if it weren't for the fact that he'd re-open up the wound on his foot that had just been sutured. He gritted his teeth and shook his head. The weapons lockout was a major setback. And he needed a major comeback. One that would make it appear as if forgetting to update the weapons systems during the transition from MilSec to UASA was on purpose.

J.A.Q.i," Cook said aloud.

"Yes, Mister President?"

"Ping Doctor Rossler."

"His status is set to Do Not Disturb—"

"GET ME THE GODDAMN DOCTOR!" The President barked.

A tone sounded. And then another. And then a third. There was no response.

"Turn on every light and screen in his home. And activate the alarm system," Cook said.

"Mr. President, I don't—"

"--National emergency. Do it."

After a few seconds, a groggy Dr. Rossler answered the pings sent by the President. "What the hell...who is this?" he asked blearily.

"It's the President of the United American State," Cook answered from his bed.

"Uh…yes, sir!" Rossler said, suddenly sounding much more awake. "It's an honor to speak with you, sir! I'm sorry, I'm still waking—"

"Cain," the President interrupted. "What is his status?"

"Well, sir, he's in critical, but stable condition," Rossler replied. "His healing trajectory puts him in the acceptable range. He's no Corta, but despite that, I do think we can work with him, sir."

"Timeframe?"

"Well, there're skin grafts, and the implant procedure, and then rehab.He suffered major spinal damage, so he's going to have to learn how to walk again. But I think—"

"How long, doctor?" the President asked.

"Twelve months…maybe eighteen."

"You have four hours," Cook stated.

"Four HOURS?!?" Doctor Rossler said in shock.. "I… I can't…"

"I suggest you get started. Right now. Call whomever you need. Bring them in. You get that man battle ready, and you do it today. *Now.*"

"But, sir!" Rossler demurred. "Project Phoenix is a three-month procedure on its own! You saw it with Corta -- and she was nowhere near as badly injured as Cain—"

"Then skip Project Phoenix," Cook snapped. "Wire his brain to a tank and cover it in spikes if you have to. I need that man up and on the battlefield by tonight!"

"Sir, I--"

"That'll be all, Doctor," President Cook said as he gestured in the air, terminating the call.

"Ping Corta."

A tone sounded.

"Yes, sir?" Major Sabrina Corta answered.

"Are you ready?" The President asked.

"Absolutely, sir," Corta replied. "Just give the order."

"It's given," Cook replied. "I'm sending something else that should help."

"But I can handle her on my own," Corta argued.

"I have no doubt," Cook answered. "You're getting it anyway."

"But, sir--"

"Godspeed, Major."

"...Yes sir," Corta responded and the connection dropped.

Cook sat at the edge of his bed and contemplated his reality. He raised his injured foot to his knee and examined it. What was once a gaping wound was now just a large scab just to the right of his plantar ligament. He examined his bedroom. The floors were spotless, save for a small red stain that the drones weren't able to tackle. Missing was the chair that was once next to his writing desk, a lamp, the glasses and trays and decanter from the drink cart (which was once again upright), and a clear view of the NewsFeed still glowing through a cracked and spiderwebbed screen.

"J.A.Q.i, turn everything off. And no calls for at least two hours."

"Yes, sir," J.A.Q.i replied as the lights dimmed.

"And I am going to need some AMP when I wake up. I've got a long day ahead of me."

"Yes, sir," J.A.Q.i said. A final tone sounded, barely audible over the rustling of the sheets as Cook slid himself into bed.

22: Sweet Dreams

Marlowe felt a light breeze drag lazily across her exposed arms. Regulations stated that she wasn't supposed to roll up her sleeves while in uniform, but it was such a lovely day, she just couldn't help herself. She also couldn't help but notice how much she'd been smiling lately. Things like light breezes, and rain storms, and even the new heat cycle meant to more closely emulate what summer had really felt like before the war…little things that she had never cared about before suddenly delighted her.

Marlowe still didn't really understand how Imagen had the ability to create things like breezes. A young Enviroscience Division officer had tried explaining it to her once during a NewsFeed roundtable discussing the latest public beta of the Environmental Atmospheric Operating System. She had cut him off famously: "When your office is the scorched glass sands of the Gaslands, things like breezes are luxuries." The clip had immediately gone viral.

Breezes, partly cloudy skies, and the new thunder and lightning cycles…despite her hardscrabble history, she had to admit: eaOS 11 was by far the best update Imagen had ever released.

Marlowe inhaled deeply and held it, doing her best to freeze this moment of time in her mind. The smell of wood on fire in a brick oven enhanced the smell of pepperoni and melted cheese and perfectly charred crust. Her stomach rumbled. She was starving. True, it was rare that she wasn't ever *not* hungry. But right then, the wine was amplifying her body's craving for both food and the touch of her love's hand. She satisfied the second by reaching out and delicately resting her hand on top of Amanda's. Marlowe locked eyes with her as she pulled Amanda's hand toward her and kissed it lightly. Essence of cucumber blended with honey as Amanda's fragrant body cream filled her nostrils. It was as intoxicating as the wine. More so, even.

A blue bubble appeared in the lower-right panel of the HUD in Marlowe's augmented eyes. It contained a comment from an anonymous viewer, reading, "BORING!" Marlowe chuckled. Her attention shifted to the ticker displaying her bank's credits balance, pinned in the lower left of her eye screens. It showed a brand-new deposit.

"Someone thinks we're boring enough that they paid the hundred-credit comment fee to tell us," Marlowe said to Amanda with a laugh.

Amanda smiled. "You know you're famous when you can charge for comments on your Feed and people actually pay to tell you it's boring," she said. She stared into the lens of the MilSec-issued body camera on Marlowe's chest and chirped, "Thanks for buying dinner!"

"What can I say?" Marlowe asked as she reached for her wine glass. "Even my boredom is profitable!"

"Cheers to that!" Amanda said, raising her glass to Marlowe. A bright *TINK*! rang out as they tapped rims.

Wine was the one vice Marlowe still allowed herself – and even then, only one glass with dinner. Viewing everything through a fog of scotch and cigar smoke tended to dull the shine of everyday life, making it hard to notice the little glints of brilliance that were the simple things. Since she'd met Amanda, however, she'd traded booze and smoke for being high on life. She'd retired from "Next Top Soldier" as a three-time champion, withdrew from foreign service, opting instead for local duty in Atlanta. According to FeedMeter, the viewership of her Feed had fallen below twenty million for the first time since she'd started streaming as an enlisted private (but was still higher than the number-two feed, NewsFeed, by nearly double). Hashtags like #MarlowesBoring, #MKingMeSleep, and #AmandaKilledMarlowe dominated NewsFeed tickers.

She didn't care.

The love of one woman had more than replaced the attention of forty million United American State citizens. Not that they all hated her – far from it. Her ratings proved that she still had half the country as a fan base. But there was no denying that her ratings had declined over the past year. The lack of engagement threw the nation's leadership into a tizzy. Imagen was actively test-marketing new potential star soldiers, casting marginally famous faces for "Next Top Soldier" and attempting to find new ways to boost the WarFeed ratings with live-streams of special invasions. The Antarctica special had come close to Marlowe's lowest ratings, but that had only resulted in the discovery of a few camps of natives and some rusted wreckage from when the International Space Station had crashed back to Earth. Even President Cook had taken to discussing Marlowe's sagging numbers during his weekly CookTalks, suggesting not so subtly that he may have to ask her to surrender her "Next Top Soldier" medals for violating the "Honor Code of serving the United American State" by "failing her duties to her fans, the citizens." He'd even hinted that he might force her back into foreign duty to get her ratings back up.

They were empty threats, of course. No non-felon could be forced to serve outside of the United American State borders, and even the President wouldn't violate The Constitution 2.0. And no one could accuse the second-most decorated soldier in MilSec history of dereliction of duty just for going out to dinner.

Her relationship with Amanda had changed her, and she couldn't deny that it was for the better. She might be boring the nation, annoying the Imagen Board of Directors, and even pissing off the President, but it just didn't matter to Marlowe. Love will do that to you. And for the first time in her life, Marlowe Kana was happy.

"Your margherita pie, madams," J.A.Q.i said as a red-checkered service drone with an Antico Pizza logo hovered its way over to their table. Three legs emerged from the bottom of the bot as it slowly lowered itself to the table.

"Oh man, that smells sooooo good," Marlowe said as she reached for a slice.

"Careful!" Amanda warned. "You're gonna burn your tongue again!"

"It's not THAT hotttfffffaaaaahhh! OW!" Marlowe yelped, pulling a triangle of pizza from her mouth, tendrils of cheese dangling.

"Are you okay?" Amanda asked with a chuckle as she dipped the edge of a cloth napkin into her water glass and handed it to Marlowe.

"Yeah," Marlowe replied as she dabbed her burnt tongue with the damp cloth. "Thanks."

"I hope there's no lasting damage," Amanda added demurely. "I'm going to need you to use that later."

Marlowe smirked from behind the napkin. Amanda returned the smile from behind her wine glass. The two held each other's eyes for that kind of eternity that only lasts a moment.
"What is it?" Amanda finally asked from behind her wine glass

"Nothing, just…" Marlowe replied, ducking her eyes and dropping the napkin on the table. She reached out both of her hands and beckoned Amanda to extend hers. Their fingertips interlaced over the middle of the table. "I'm happy," Marlowe said.

"Me, too," Amanda replied. She whispered it again. And again. "Me too… Me too… Me too…"

Amanda's voice began to echo as she repeated the phrase. Marlowe narrowed her eyes. The entire world around her began to glow, as if someone had turned the brightness up well past the maximum setting in her HUD. The world blurred and turned bright red. Tendrils of dark red snaked around her field of vision like roots from a tree. They moved left, and then right, and then back to center. A small slit of light split the horizon. Light flooded in and the world turned a bright blue-white as she realized she could hear the characteristic whirr of Jumper rotors.

"She's awake," she heard Austin's voice say from her left.

"Don't move, Marlowe," The Judge's voice said from her right.

"Stay very, very still," Jen added from directly in front of her.

"What's happening?" Marlowe asked groggily.

"What's the last thing you remember?" The Judge asked.

"That your moustache is cheesy," Marlowe said. "And that I hate you."

The Judge laughed. "Well, she's still herself," he said. "That counts for something. Good work, Austin."

"Thank you, sir," Austin responded. "Just a few more seconds, and…there. I'm out. I'll pull the plug."

"What plug?" Marlowe asked. "Wait…did you..."

"Please, Marlowe, stay calm," Jen urged desperately.

Marlowe slowly reached her left hand up to the scarred area just behind her left ear. She felt a wire dangling from the spot where she'd yanked her Pod out while in prison, removing in very dramatic fashion the device that had once connected her to J.A.Q.i before it was overwritten with PrisonOS. She traced the wire forward and felt it connecting to the back of a portable terminal in front of Austin.

"Motherfucker!" she yelled in fury. Austin's eyes bulged from their sockets as Marlowe seized him by the neck.

"NO!" Jen yelled, grabbing Marlowe's arm.

"He jack-hacked me!" Marlowe seethed.

"URK," Austin squeaked.

"We didn't have a choice!" Jen insisted. "You were completely out. We had to move fast!"

Still clutching Austin's throat, Marlowe locked eyes with Jen. "*We?* You mean you *allowed* this?!?" She asked her sister, mouth agape in disbelief.

"You were bugged!" Jen said, doubling her effort to pull Marlowe's arm back. "Hax's virus…not only did it override your muscular control, it turned your entire system into an antenna! Every single near-field communication beacon pinged off of you! That's how MilSec found us!"

"They're the Army now," Nines corrected from nearby.

"Shut up!" Jen snapped as she whipped her head around.

"Stop being wrong and I will!" Nines retorted.

"Your sister and Nines both watched the entire time," the Judge calmly told Marlowe. "You were not violated in any way. In fact, if you let Austin go, he has some good news for you."

"HUKKKK," Austin gurgled in response.

Jen looked back at her sister. "Please," she begged Marlowe. "Let him go."

Marlowe gritted her teeth and released her grip. Austin choked and gasped for air.

"So dramatic," the Judge said. "Why can't you just accept help from people? We are on your side, Marlowe."

"You're on your own side," Marlowe replied as she turned to face the Judge. "You made that clear. And no one — NO ONE — violates me like that. You agreed."

"I said nothing installed," the Judge replied. "Nothing was installed. Austin simply stripped the bug, and he repaired your targeting system while he was at it."

Marlowe blinked. She stared at the Judge's face and realized that it was covered in a very light green mesh. A rangefinder in the bottom right of her field of vision indicated that his head was swaying between twenty-five and twenty-six inches away from her face.

"But… how…"

"You don't…need J.A.Q.i…for telemetry," Austin croaked as he gingerly rubbed his throat. "They just attach it for logs and data mining."

"Your on-board system is restored," the Judge said. "Be thankful."

"...Thanks," Marlowe grumbled. "But all things considered, I'd rather you'd just discussed all of this with me first and asked for my consent."

"We're at war," the Judge replied. "You're a weapon. We upgraded you while removing a threat to our survival. You of all people must understand that."

Marlowe sat up and rubbed her temples, blinking a few times. She looked up toward the cockpit of the Jumper and saw Poet in the gunner's seat, with Angel in the co-pilot seat and Angel's younger doppleganger from the EV plant flying in the pilot's chair. Nines was squatting between the two pilots, taking in the view as the team approached the brightening Atlanta skyline. She glanced left at Austin, and then right at her sister. Everything she observed was wrapped in thin, tactical mesh, with sensitive areas of each human body glowing a faint red. Distances for each highlighted object popped up in a table in the bottom-right of her view.

She shook her head. "I feel violated," she said.

"You're going to feel a lot worse than that in a second," Jen said with a sigh. "You're not going to like where we're headed."

Marlowe's face went flat. "And where is that?" she asked.

"Amanda's," Jen answered quietly.

"NO." Marlowe said. "I'm out. This is ridiculous."

"It's our only play," The Judge replied. "We've got to find that footage and—"

"Then *find* it!" Marlowe snapped. "Go to a library! Or an Imagen Coffee hotspot! Hell, you have three hackers on board, why can't we just bust in and take it from any of a thousand other places?"

"We can do that, but what then?" The Judge replied. "We have to get it out to the public, and fast."

Marlowe's eyes widened and she gestured dramatically at Nines. "We have MKFan_9999 RIGHT HERE!" she yelled.

"We need NewsFeed," Jen mumbled, head lowered in shame. "We need Amanda."

Marlowe stared holes into the top of Jen's head, silently insisting that she look up and face her. Jen felt her unspoken demand and complied.

"How could you?" Marlowe asked. "You tried to turn me in, and you know what? I can forgive that. You just let me get jack-hacked, and I can even forgive *that*. But dragging me—in my sleep—to Amanda's?"

"Get over it," The Judge said. "We're going. Put this on." He reached out and proffered Marlowe a Dazzle-camouflaged bandanna they were all wearing.

"Why the costumes?"

"It disrupts facial recognition. It works, trust me."

"Poet told me. But I'm pretty sure it won't help. Me, at least."

"Why?" Nines asked as she reluctantly tied the bandanna around her face.

"My weight, my density…there aren't many four-hundred-pound women under six feet tall running around with metal muscles."

"We're coming in from the roof," The Judge said. "Floor sensors will be minimal."

"That puts us on radar!" Marlowe said. "We'll be shot down before we even get to the building."

"Seraph is a very gifted pilot," The Judge said indicating Angel's sister.

"Gifted or not, no one can outfly the air-defense matrix," Marlowe insisted.

"She doesn't have to," The Judge replied. "All she has to do is fly like a Zifty."

"...A food taxi?" Marlowe asked.

"Yep," the Judge replied. "We've hacked the Jumper's registry so that we identify as a ZiftyDelivery. It won't pass a visual, but it'll keep the automated defenses from firing."

Marlowe scowled. Reluctantly, she reached out and grabbed the bandanna. She sighed as she tied it around her neck, ready to pull it up over her face.

"You don't have to face her," Jen offered, placing her hand on Marlowe's shoulder. "I'll go in. You can wait on the roof."

"She can," The Judge said, his smirk returning. "But she won't."

Marlowe's eyes shot up, brimming with anger. She wanted to tell The Judge that he was wrong. She wanted to throw him from the Jumper. She wanted to go back to sleep. She wanted to go back in time.

She lowered her gaze back to the deck of the transport. She couldn't deny that he was right.

Everyone on board the Jumper found themselves in the midst of an awkward silence. Seraph kept the hovering vehicle safely in the drone lanes of Atlanta's airspace, obeying the speed limit while flying and cornering in exact lines. Marlowe found herself secretly hoping that the registry hack would fail and the automated turrets atop every building would open fire and send the Jumper streaking from the sky into the side of Amanda's building, killing only the evil ex-girlfriend who had crushed Marlowe's heart into a billion irreparable pieces. She couldn't help but imagine a sharp-eyed soldier spotting the Jumper and shooting a grappling hook to its strut and boarding, engaging her in a fight, betraying their cover and forcing them to flee. She even thought about grabbing an emergency jump chute from the bay and leaping from the craft and disappearing into the charred remains of the Subs until she could amass enough scavenged supplies to flee across the Mississippi River into the deadlands of the American west, living as a nomad and surviving on her wits and the occasional lucky catch of a mutated cat--

"--We're here," Seraph announced from the pilot's seat.

Marlowe's stomach swirled. All of her mental capacity focused on trying not to vomit what little remained of the Battery bars she'd had the night before.

"Bring her down just beside the drone landing pad," The Judge ordered. "Last thing we need is a Jumper's interrupted landing tipping anyone off."

23. Ex Marks The Spot

Angel, Seraph, Poet, and Austin waited in the Jumper while Marlowe, Nines, Jen, and the Judge took the rooftop stairway down a floor to Amanda's penthouse apartment complex. Not a word was said as they entered the hallway and approached a door marked 45-1. The Judge knocked smartly on the door several times.

The moment that the door opened, Marlowe caught a hint of Amanda's perfume in the air. A thousand moth-like memories danced around the fire of her thoughts. She wanted to bolt down the hallway and out of the building and run as fast and as far as she could to somewhere...anywhere.

But she couldn't leave. The stakes were too high.

She stood fast as The Judge led the way into Amanda's apartment...*Amanda's apartment*. She mentally spat at the thought. Amanda would never have been approved for that space without Marlowe. In fact, Amanda hadn't contributed a single credit for the place until several months after Marlowe left...the night everything went south. After that night, Marlowe couldn't stand the thought of staying there, yet couldn't bring herself to have Amanda evicted either. Despite Amanda's affair, she just couldn't force herself to be that vindictive.

How fucking stupid I was, she thought as Jen walked in behind The Judge. *This woman has made an entire career out of making me into a heel on NewsFeed. Never mind everything I did for her, or everything I didn't do to her that I could have!* She shook her head, steeling herself. She inhaled in a deep breath and took a step forward, colliding directly with Nines, who was standing halfway in the doorway.

"Watch out!" Nines barked. "What the hell?"

"...Sorry," Marlowe said. She looked at Nines, who looked back at her in irritation. "...Going in?" Marlowe asked slowly.

"Personal space, man..." Nines muttered, suddenly seeming all of fifteen years old. She stepped forward through the doorway, then sauntered over by Jen who was busy surveying the apartment.

Marlowe blinked and shook her head, annoyed. But upon glimpsing Amanda sitting expectantly in her living room, all thoughts of Nines and her teenage angst left, and Marlowe's mind became a roaring blank.

Marlowe walked past The Judge, Jen, Nines, and Amanda with her eyes glued to the runner rug. She pulled out one of the dining chairs she had picked out with Amanda three years prior and plopped herself into it.

The air sat thick with tension for almost thirty seconds. The Judge cleared his throat once. Everyone looked his way to see what he was going to say. He shrugged. "Sorry…throat's dry."

Amanda forced a nervous chuckle. Another awkward tension threatened to take up residence when Jen finally broke the silence.

"Nice shirt," she said, pulling her own shirt down to resemble Amanda's extremely low-cut blouse. "Ratings low?"

"Not anymore, thanks to your sister," Amanda said coolly. "They're at an all-time high."

"Well, I'm sure viewers are thoroughly entertained," Jen snapped.

Amanda smirked. "At least I'm not dressed like the world's most ridiculous chessboard. What's with the masks?"

"Necessity," Jen said. "We don't want to wear this stuff, but we have to. Just like we don't want to be here, but we have to–Nines, put that down!"

The solid chink of glass-on-glass echoed throughout the room as Nines clumsily lowered a small porcelain statue of a dog back to its place on an end table. "I'm bored," she complained as she plopped down on the RealLeather couch that dominated the room. "This sucks."

"Necessary evil," Jen said. "Sit still and let the adults talk, okay, sweetheart?"

"Eat a dick," Nines huffed. She pulled out the Pod that Marlowe had given her and buried her face in it. The Judge chuckled and took a seat next to her. Nines glared in his direction. She scooted herself closer to the armrest and returned to hacking the planet.

"Yeahhhhh…so…" Amanda drawled, dragging her words out for maximum effect. "When are you going to get around to telling me why you're here?"

Jen looked over at the Judge, who was smirking.

"…You going to tell her?" Jen asked.

He softly closed his eyes and shrugged, and then nodded toward Jen, insisting that she do the honors.

"Welllll, okay then," Jen said with a heavy sigh, "You *know* why we're here, I'm sure. Or else we wouldn't be here."

"I want to hear you say it," Amanda said with a satisfied smirk on her face. "I want you to ask for my help."

"And I want to watch the light leave your eyes while I choke you to death," Jen retorted. "And yet, here I sit, behaving myself and doing what's necessary to deal with the situation at hand. I was assured by mister 'The Judge' here that you'd cooperate."

"I'll cooperate, but I want you to ask."

Jen ground her molars and glared at Amanda, whose smirk deepened. She then looked at the Judge, whose own smirk she thought couldn't have possibly deepened, somehow had.

"What the fuck, dude?!" Jen shouted at him. "I didn't sign up for this!"

"And yet, here you are," the Judge replied, still grinning wickedly.

"Motherfucker…" Jen shook her head, took another deep breath in through her nostrils, and finally asked through clenched teeth, "Will you help us?"

"Why won't Marlowe ask me?" Amanda asked. She glanced over toward the dining room area where Marlowe sat, head dramatically turned away. "She's the one who needs the help. *She* should ask. Hell, I'd even settle for a simple 'hello' at this point."

"I'm not sure if you've had a chance to watch the playback of your own show this morning, but she's had a pretty busy day."

"No need to remind me," Amanda said. "Hell of a show she's put on."

"Might even keep you on NewsFeed for another month," Jen snapped. "Oh wait, you're fucking your producer. You don't need things like story or content, do you?"

Amanda's smirk faded. She looked over at The Judge. "You really expect me to take this?" She asked.

The Judge appeared to be struggling not to laugh.

"Look," Jen said, trying to pull the quickly unraveling moment back together. "Marlowe's really tired. We all are. It's been a long day, as you know. And the sooner we can get things rolling and get this over with, the better."

"What are you, her interpreter?"

"I'm her sister!" Jen barked, losing the little composure she'd regained. "And you're the bitch who keeps dragging her name through the mud and, oh you know...ruined her life. So you'll have to understand that she may not have much to say to you."

"I'd argue that the attempted murder and subsequent jailbreak has done far more to ruin her life than any ex-girlfriend could," Amanda said. "And I'm not dragging her name through the mud. It's the job. It's all performance. You know that and she knows that. I've tried to apologize, but how can I? She won't accept my pings. She obviously has me blocked."

"Deservedly so," Jen answered. "It's for the best. Trust me, you don't want to hear anything she'd have to say. It's all pretty unflattering."

"Ooh! I do!" Nines chirped, her gaze lifting from the Pod screen.

Jen glared at Nines. Nines looked down and quickly resumed her activities on the Pod.

"Well, the same could be said about the things she told me about you," Amanda jibed, bringing Jen's focus back to her. "Unflattering would be the mildest way to describe it."

"Yeah, I'm sure," Jen replied. "I've done some dumb shit, and will probably do even more. But we're sisters. We *get* to hate each other. It's in the contract. You, however? You're just some low-rent stripper who fucked her way to the middle."

"What's wrong with stripping?" Nines asked, re-engaged.

"Goddammit, Nines! Stay out of this!" Jen snapped.

"It's a noble profession!" Nines yelled.

"Quite!" Amanda agreed, bestowing on Jen a triumphant glare.

Jen was momentarily taken aback. "Wait, you're going to count her opinion as vindication?" She asked Amanda. "She's twelve!"

"Fifteen!" Nines corrected. "And that doesn't mean I'm not right!"

"Who cares?!?" Jen shouted.

"I do," Amanda said. "Let the kid speak."

"I'm not a kid, you bitch," Nines replied. "And stripping is a noble profession."

Amanda smirked. "Cute kid. I like her."

"Well, I hate you!" Nines barked as she raised her eyes and locked them on Amanda. "Your show is the lowest-rated piece of shit ever broadcast on any Feed, ever, in history. And deservedly so, because it's shit. It's really shitty shit. My worst-performing automated scripts make better-edited story footage than your entire production team. You used Marlowe to get a show you don't deserve and and everyone knows it. You're terrible and I hate your stupid face."

Amanda was taken aback. She turned to Jen. "Who's the brat?" she asked.

"She's got the evidence I told you about," The Judge said, finally speaking up.

"NOW you choose to talk?" Jen said incredulously.

"It wasn't my turn before," The Judge said. "Now it is. Amanda, may we please have the password to your NetNode?"

"Don't need it," Nines said without looking up, tapping away on the Pod. "I guessed it on the third try. Pro tip, Amanda. Zeroes instead of the letter 'o' in Marlowe? Not *really* secure."

"Well, goody," Jen said with mock glee. "The sooner we find that footage, the sooner we get the hell out of here."

"Sorry my apartment isn't up to your lavish standards, Subbie," Amanda sneered.

"I *like* the Subs. They're honest and I earn my place there," Jen retorted

"You don't think I earned this?" Amanda said.

"Sure," Jen sneered, "You *earned* it by fucking your way here! You fucked Marlowe to get famous, and then fucked her again when you cheated on her with your producer to get the slot on NewsFeed, and then–"

There was a sudden crash as Marlowe's fist went clear through the dining room table. Splintered wood clattered against the linoleum and chair legs screeched against the floor as Marlowe stood. "ENOUGH!" she screamed.

Everyone's attention snapped toward Marlowe. Nines raised her Pod and snapped a quick photo of Marlowe standing amongst the shattered wreckage of fine dining fixtures.

"Nines," Marlowe groaned. "Erase that."

"Nope." Nines replied without looking up.

Marlowe sighed. "Look, this sucks, okay?" she said as she stalked toward the kitchenette. "No one in this apartment wants to be here right now. Least of all me, for at least two very huge, equally depressing reasons. But we are here. We have a mission." She opened the door to a cabinet, scanned the contents, and closed it before opening another.

"Top right, next to the sink," Amanda said without looking up.

Marlowe froze as if lightning had zapped through her body. Her cheeks smoldered and fire burned the tips of her ears. Of all the things she'd imagined Amanda saying to her if they ever met again, "Top right, next to the sink" wasn't even in the top ten thousand. This was the first time Amanda had spoken to her in over a year and a half. She wanted to kill her. She wanted to grab her and hold her in her arms and not let her go. She wanted to throw her through the wall. She wanted to disappear through the floor. More than anything, she wanted to suddenly wake up and realize that the last nineteen months of her life had been a very terrible dream, wipe the cold sweat from her brow, roll over, and go back to sleep where better dreams awaited.

Breathing slowly, she managed to regain her composure. She opened the aforementioned cabinet, retrieved a glass, and put it under the water dispenser. A quick jet of water shot into the glass.

"...Thank you," Marlowe said to Amanda.

"...You're welcome," Amanda replied reluctantly. "Look, Marlowe, I am really–"

"AT ANY RATE," Marlowe interrupted. "Nines is locating footage that proves I didn't attack Corta first and was actually acting out of self-defense." She took a gulp of water from the glass and wiped her mouth, then walked around the corner of the kitchen into the living room.

Amanda opened her mouth to say something, but appeared dumbfounded.

Marlowe continued. "Mister moustache over there assured me that you are willing to leak this footage and help clear my name and get my father out of prison. Is that the deal?"

"Well, I promised I'd air the footage, but–"

"Is that the goddamn deal or not!?" Marlowe asked.

Silence. Then "...Yes," The Judge finally answered for Amanda. "Everything I promised will be--"

"I want to hear *her* say it!" Marlowe barked, pointing at Amanda. "Yes or no!"

Amanda stared at Marlowe for a few seconds. She nodded.

"Fucking *say* it," Marlowe demanded.

"Yes," Amanda squeaked.

"Good enough for me," Marlowe said, setting the empty glass down, before striding for the door. "I'm done here. If you need me, I'll be in the Jumper. Let me know when Nines finds the footage."

"Wait. Marlowe!" Amanda called out.

Marlowe willed herself not to stop, but her body betrayed her. She froze just short of the hallway leading toward the door.

"I...I'm sorry. Truly," Amanda said earnestly. She let out a deep sigh. "I've had years to think this over, and I just...I know I didn't treat you fairly--"

"--*Fairly*?" Jen snapped. "Fairly is a pipe dream compared to what you've done! You've made her life a living hell!"

"Jen, I got this," Marlowe said half-heartedly.

"Marlowe, just tonight she called you a menace on the air at least five times!"

"Twelve," Nines said, still focused on the Pod.

Everyone turned to look at Nines. "My scripts automatically highlight keywords and hashtags," Nines explained. "They make supercuts of Amanda saying stupid things. It's an endless supply of credits. I just posted tonight's video. I didn't just sit here and count them or anything. I'm not a psycho. Quit looking at me."

The room was silent for a moment. Marlowe turned and began marching down the hallway toward the door.

"Wait!" Amanda said, standing up and rushing toward Marlowe. "I want to make this up to you!" She darted past Marlowe and cut her off in the middle of the hallway. "That's why I agreed when the Judge approached me! I see it as a chance to make everything up to you. I really do. I just...I have a career and a persona I have to maintain! You understand, right? It's just for engagement! Viewers respond to it! Like…like what your little friend just said. It's about keywords and hashtags! You understand that, right? And so I have to do things like call you a menace! It's for work! I need you to understand that. I need you to know that I am truly, truly sorry. You meant the world to me and I made a huge mistake."

Marlowe looked up and locked eyes with Amanda. Amanda tried to to look away, and almost did, but stopped herself from breaking eye contact. She took a step toward Marlowe.

"You believe me, right?" she asked, reaching out and taking Marlowe's hands.

Jen sighed loudly, clearly disgusted. The Judge was studying Marlowe and Amanda with fascination. Amanda leaned in toward Marlowe with pleading eyes. Marlowe could taste metal. She wanted both to kiss and kill Amanda. Her teeth unclenched. Her lips parted. She began to speak.

"Found it!" Nines yelled, breaking the tension.

Everyone flinched. They turned toward Nines. "Yep," she said, flipping the Pod around so Marlowe could see it. "You were right. She ambushed you."

"...I know I was right," Marlowe said, dropping Amanda's hands. "I was there." She pushed past Amanda and walked toward the door.

"Where are you going?" The Judge asked. "We just found what we--"

"--Getting some air," Marlowe answered. "You guys have a lot of work to do. I need a minute. Amanda, unlock the door."

"Wait, we still--"

"I'm going through that door in three seconds," Marlowe stated grimly. "It's your choice as to how much cleaning up you want to do when I leave."

"I don't want you to leave!" Amanda yelled. "I want to work this out! I want us to be okay!"

"Okay?!" Marlowe snapped, spinning to face Amanda. "Look around you! This used to be my *life*! That sofa… those chairs…that table I just smashed! We picked those together. We made this place what it is. And you went and ruined it ALL!" Marlowe's eyes narrowed and her tone became dour. "But *you're* okay, aren't you? You still get to live in this reality. Hell, you even moved the glasses to the

80

cabinet you fought me over! Meanwhile, I still have to live in a reality I don't understand, and I understand it less and less as the days go by. I fight my way through it blind, while you get paid to critique me as I do it in spite of -- or rather, *because* of how well you know me. Now open the goddamn door."

Amanda stared at the floor. She inhaled deeply. "J.A.Q.i, open the door," she ordered. A tone sounded, and the latches binding the door to the frame retracted.

Marlowe turned and grabbed the doorknob. She held it fast. "Do you remember our song?" Marlowe asked over her shoulder.

"'Beautiful Her,'" Amanda said immediately without looking up from the floor.

"When you hear that song, does all the air leave your lungs and you double over in pain as tears and snot drip all over the floor? Or is that just me?"

Amanda blinked a few times. She began to answer, but it was a little too late.

"Thought so," Marlowe said as she opened the door, passed through it, and gently closed it behind her.

"You told me she'd be receptive," Amanda said to The Judge after a moment's stunned silence from the group.

"That *was* receptive," Jen interjected. "You're not dead or nursing a black eye. Consider that an agreement."

The Judge nodded. "You don't need her to like you. You just need her to be on board. And I have to agree with Jen. The fact that the only thing broken in here is a table is, I think, getting off light."

Amanda shook her head and walked over to the couch. She fell into it as if knocked off her feet by the emotional strain. "I'm not doing this," Amanda said numbly.

Jen snarled. "Bitch, you're airing that footage, or so help me--"

"--May I remind you of the very considerable leverage I have on you?" The Judge added with some menace. "Society may not care about your gender reassignment and Marlowe's very understanding. Your producer boyfriend, however...your ratings don't go up if you don't have a show."

Amanda glared at The Judge. "Of course. You don't have to remind me," she snarled. "I'm *very* aware."

Jen's jaw dropped. "Wait...your producer doesn't know? But I thought everyone knew..."

"Just because Marlowe told her sister doesn't mean the world is privy to every aspect of our lives," Amanda said. "It's my business."

"Then you'll abandon this little pity party and fulfill your end of our agreement?" The Judge said.

Amanda nodded reluctantly.

"Great. Nines, get--" Amanda began.

"Aw, not you, too!" Nines snapped. "My name is Regina!"

"Why does everyone call you Nines then?"

"She's MKFan_9999," Jen said as she stood to leave. "You figure it out. In fact, you three figure all the rest of this out. I don't need to be here for that. I'm going to get some air with Marlowe." She looked at Amanda and gestured toward the doorway. "Do you mind?"

"Gladly," Amanda replied. "J.A.Q.i, open the door."

Jen left and the door locked behind her. Nines scooted over to Amanda on the couch to show her the footage. "You have an editing setup here?" Nines asked. "If not, I can do it all on this."

"...So you're the FeedLeech making all those Marlowe videos?" Amanda asked. "Wow...I thought you were a man."

"Looks like we both have identity issues," Nines said. "We doing this or what?"

The Judge leaned back in his seat and smiled.

———

Jen pushed the manual lever on the doorway leading to the roof. She saw the Jumper just in front of her and Marlowe leaning on a railing looking out to the city just beyond. Jen breathed in deeply and approached the Jumper.

"Do I even wanna know what happened?" Poet asked from the gunner's chair.

Jen shrugged. "We got the footage and it's going live," she said. "All it cost was that moment right there." She nodded toward the cockpit. Through the front windscreen, Poet saw Marlowe leaning against the railing that separated the rooftop from a thirty-eight story drop down to Peachtree Street.

"Good luck," Poet said with a rueful smile. Jen nodded, then left and joined Marlowe. Marlowe kept her gaze on the morning sky over the city. Without saying a word, Jen handed over a lighter and a cigar she had pulled from the go-bag they'd brought from Jen's apartment.

"Thanks," Marlowe said and took the items without looking. She placed the cap of the cigar between her front teeth and bit into the tobacco wrapper, ripping a thin layer from the very tip of the cigar.

"You okay?"

"Not even slightly," Marlowe answered.

"You wanna talk about it?" Jen asked.

Marlowe took a deep drag from her cigar. She chambered the smoke in her mouth for a moment, savoring the flavors. She pursed her lips. A steady chimney-like smoke plume poured from it. "I hate her. You know I hate her. I hated being in the room with her. I hated asking for a favor from her. She sucks so, so much, to say the very least, and I know you hate her, too," Marlowe said. "But leave the noble profession of stripping out of it."

Jen laughed, caught off guard but relieved to see her sister not completely destroyed. "It's depraved, using your tits for money," she said with a smile.

"Isn't that your favorite tactic in poker?" Marlowe asked. "Wearing some low-cut thing and leaning forward so the green gamblers can get an eyeful?"

"Hey, that's poker," Jen answered, reaching out and gesturing toward Marlowe's cigar. Marlowe shrugged and handed it to her. "All's fair in cards and crusades," Jen continued. "What can I say? People don't think straight when they're horny. But at least there's honor in how I do it."

"How so?"

Jen held up the cigar and examined the lit end. She contemplated its glowing red embers, rolling the stick in her fingertips. "One's a game," she said calmly. "The other is a way of life."

"Poker is how you pay your rent," Marlowe stated. "You literally live off gambling."

"But I don't live off tips from showing my tits."

Marlowe chuckled. Her gaze left the city skyline as she finally found the wherewithal to look at her sister. "You're seriously fucking broken, you know that?"

"Says the augmented super soldier wearing forty pounds of steel around her wrists and ankles after breaking out of prison for attempted murder," Jen said, bringing the cigar to her lips for a puff. She took a dramatic drag, and immediately began coughing violently. A stream of smoke poured from her mouth and nose as she doubled over, gagging.

"You're not supposed to inhale!" Marlowe said through her laughter. She patted her sister gently on the back and helped her stand. "Deep breaths…there you go…"

"Why the hell...do you like...those things?" Jen gasped, fighting for air.

"Refined tastes, I suppose – wait, where'd it go?"

Jen coughed while pointing over the railing of the apartment building.

"Shit," Marlowe said as her shoulders slumped forward and her head sagged. "Waste of a good Cuesta."

Marlowe and Jen both jumped as the stairway access door slammed open. "We have to go!" The Judge barked as he rushed through the door, Nines following closely behind.

"What happened?" Marlowe yelled as she jogged toward the Jumper. Jen trotted along behind her.

"You didn't see the NewsFeed alert?" The Judge asked. "Wait, no, of course you didn't. Jen? You didn't get an alert?"

"None," Jen croaked.

"Poet?" The Judge asked as he climbed into the vehicle. "Alerts?"

"Nothing on NewsFeed or any of the main CitizenFeeds," Poet replied, reaching out a hand to help Jen in.

"Good, it's not out there yet," The Judge said. "We can still beat it. Seraph, spool up and take off!" Seraph saluted from the cockpit and began flipping switches on the console before her.

"Beat what?" Marlowe asked as she helped Nines into the Jumper, and then climbed in behind her.

"Amanda just got the tip on a private wire feed. Cook just ordered your father's execution."

Marlowe and Jen both fell silent as the MagLev engines on the Jumper whined and whirred. The Jumper dusted off and cleared the railing of the rooftop by less than an inch, before descending in near-freefall to below radar level, and shooting off into the distance.

24. The Good Doctor

"Brow," Dr. Ben Rossler whispered from behind his sweat-soaked surgical mask.

A MediDrone extended an appendage and blew a jet of sterile air on the surgeon's forehead as he delicately attached the final lead connecting a brand new Powerhouse-class left leg augmentation to the newly installed neural gateway embedded in Henry "Mad Dog" Cain's spine. The operation was creeping into its third hour, which was longer than either the doctor or his staff had slept since racing to save Cain's life earlier in the evening. But the watchers of MedFeed knew that sleep deprivation was hardly a problem for Dr. Rossler. His staff was comprised of eleven of the best surgeons in the world (and one personal assistant), and he was an echelon well above them. Which is why no one - not the one hundred thousand citizens watching the surgery live, nor the doctor's staff, nor the President himself - had any doubt that Dr. Rossler could bring Mad Dog back to the field of battle.

Dr. Rossler, however, was secretly marveling at the progress he was able to make in the time allotted. Not because of how difficult the procedure was – he knew how good he was. And not because of the lack of sleep or the hairpin timeline that would have been impossible for any other surgeon. It was the fact that he could get any of it done with Amanda Stokes' voice blaring from all around as he dutifully followed the President's orders and performed one of the most important operations of his career.

"And she was quite serious about the threat, too," Stokes was relaying on-screen to the audience of "AM/BEAT," the early morning NewsFeed show hosted by Pat Daniels. "She swore she'd kill me and everyone else around me if I didn't broadcast this footage."

"Amanda," Pat Daniels said solemnly. "We all know you're traumatized – you've not had any sleep since your show ended its broadcast a few hours ago. Heck, one could argue that you haven't slept much in months. As your partner in the continuing coverage of the Marlowe Kana trial, I can attest to that!" He chuckled in the smarmily professional way only news anchors could achieve. Amanda smiled in response as Pat continued, "and you've just suffered through a scary confrontation. On behalf of all our viewers, thank you so much for staying up and joining us as a guest."

"It's my honor and my job," Amanda replied with a sickly smile.

Pat nodded. "But the million-credit question is: Do you believe that Marlowe Kana is telling the truth and that this footage is real?"

Amanda took a deep breath. "I think in my current state, I can't really say," she answered.

"We wish you wouldn't," Dr. Rossler muttered as he pulled on a spool of nanofiber wiring and fed it into an arterial conduit in Mad Dog's torso.

Amanda was continuing her on-screen speech. "I'm still in shock and afraid for my life after Marlowe Kana broke into my apartment and trashed it – you see this? See the table over there? She pointed to her left, and the camera drone turned to show the table that Marlowe had smashed during her visit. "That could have been me! She could have done that to me!"

"But, Amanda, certainly you have to have an opinion on her innocence or guilt, after seeing this, frankly, shocking footage of Sergeant Corta ambushing MK in the locker room." The footage began playing again in a corner window just above Pat's head. "I mean, this negates the entire treason charge right here. If this footage is real and not a holo-dupe, it means that–"

"--I can't say," Amanda interrupted. "The citizens of the United American State will have to decide for themselves. And we all can honestly say that these last twenty-four hours have been some of the darkest in our nation's history. Marlowe Kana, found guilty of treason, of all things? And a jailbreak that results in the Atlanta Subs being torched and razed? Not to mention the nationalization of MilSec and an apparent schism between our President and the corporation his family founded, which employs us all and keeps us safe. Tensions are clearly high, and the unbelievable is now commonplace. So I wouldn't blame our viewers if they feel it is possible this footage is a holo-dupe. But ask yourself…when did Marlowe Kana get time to commission a holo-dupe? She's been behind bars since the incident, until just now – and if someone could create one in just a day that looks this accurate…"

"Ugh, God, make up your mind," Dr. Rossler blurted out. "First she hates Marlowe, now she defends Marlowe… which is it?I"

"Focus, sir," Dr. Vessey, Rossler's lead assistant, urged calmly.

Amanda took a deep breath, and then looked directly into the lens. "But if we're really thinking about it…" She paused and took another deep breath for effect. "It would seem that the only entity with the resources to pull something like that off would be Imagen Corporation…"

"What would they gain?" Pat asked.

"It's a good question, isn't it?" Amanda said mysteriously.

"Well, viewers at home – in fact, the entire country – would love to know: Is this footage real? Or is it an elaborate farce perpetrated by Imagen corporation?"

"The people at home are the ones who have to decide, Pat," Amanda replied. "My judgement is honestly clouded, due to adrenaline and the fact that I'm sleep deprived."

"*You're* sleep deprived?" Dr. Rossler muttered under his breath as he attached another neural lead to the base controller of Mad Dog's new legs. "Why is this even on? J.A.Q.i, please put on some jazz."

"I cannot," J.A.Q.i replied. "NewsFeed has been pinned on all displays, unclosable."

"Well, can you please mute it?" he begged J.A.Q.i.

"Mute is not possible, but I have lowered the volume as low as I can," J.A.Q.i replied politely. "I hope that it helps."

Rossler grumbled. "Scalpel," he barked.

Vessey, placed one delicately in his hand. "Focus," she reminded him again sharply.

Dr. Rossler blinked deliberately. He inhaled deeply from his nostrils and exhaled through the damp surgical mask. This is why he paid Dr. Vessey enough to ensure she'd never leave. She knew how to navigate the fine line between respect and responsibility. It, however, still stung to have to be reminded that a human life hung in the balance between his skill and his predisposition of finding NewsFeed presenters distasteful. But he appreciated the candor. "Thank you, doctor," he replied equably.

"Of course, doc–oh my..." Vessey gasped. Doctor Rossler looked up at his lead assistant to find her eyes glued to the wall full of screens just beyond the glass wall of the surgical center.

"Here with us now is Alan Davis, Chairman of the Board for Imagen Corporation," Pat Daniels said as the screen split from two faces to three. "Now, Chairman, clearly these have been some of the most interesting hours of your career and, frankly, in our nation's history. What, exactly, is your take on Cook nationalizing MilSec and turning it into the United American State Army? And his order just a few moments ago for General Kana's execution?"

"I will be issuing a full statement on the MilSec nationalization, and many other issues, in due time," Chairman Davis replied gravely. "There is a lot to be decided, and the Board and all trustees will be considering our options and preparing our response. But one thing that has been decided, and the reason I am streaming to you live this morning, is to announce that the Board has unanimously voted for an immediate and unconditional pardon of Major Marlowe Kana, as well as her father, General Ashish Kana."

Pat Daniels and Amanda Stokes both gasped on-air, while Dr. Rossler, Dr. Vessey, ten other surgeons and assistants, and the twenty million citizens glued to the Feeds all gasped as well in near unison.

Alan Davis continued. "An Imagen judicial tribunal has been formed and the paperwork is being signed as I speak. To General Kana, I want to apologize for the false imprisonment and public display last evening, and to Major Marlowe Kana, I would personally like to extend a very heartfelt apology and a full reinstatement into MilSec, with back pay and a direct promotion to general."

"But, sir," Pat Daniel said, "There is no MilSec–"

"That is all," Alan Davis said as his Feed went black.

"Well, what a *stunning* development!" Pat Daniels brayed. "I can't believe it...MK has been pardoned!" The text crawl underneath on the screen immediately changed to repeat the news alert in all capital letters.

A tone sounded. "Doctor," J.A.Q.i stated, "NewsFeed has just been marked closable. Would you like me to--"

"Shit yes, close it!" Dr. Rossler said with relief.

"I think this little project just got deprioritized," Dr. Vessy opined. "You should take a break and let us take over."

"Well, he's sitting here wide open and half his body is augmented...I might as well finish the job," Dr. Rossler replied wearily.

Rossler returned his focus to the task at hand and completed the connections to Mad Dog's augmented right leg. One more leg, another arm, and some spinal repair to go. He would get it done, of course – and with a few hours to spare. The attention given him by a nation severely desensitized by technological advancement was not unearned. While he had been working to repair Sergeant Sabrina Corta, medical tech breakthroughs came to him daily. His simulations seemed to run at nearly twenty times their operational speed. In fact, the simulation deciphering the architecture of Marlowe Kana's nanofiber-augmented muscular system had been running for years. Then somehow, the moment he needed it to save Corta, it had found a solution to the one problem vexing Dr. Rossler: how to power nanofiber augmentations internally versus adding the augmentations to existing body parts. With that problem solved, reverse-engineering simulations based on the samples taken from Marlowe in prison took mere minutes. And now, thanks to these massive advancements, procedures to enhance the human body were limited only by the availability of the nanofiber muscle tissue, which took months to grow.

As a scientist, he couldn't help but question the timing, intent, and coincidence of such monumental technological and medical breakthroughs occurring in such a small amount of time. He couldn't help but wonder just how, exactly, a simulation that had been running for *years* could suddenly crack the mystery of Marlowe Kana's metal muscles...and just in the nick of time.

As a pragmatist, he knew better than to look a gift horse in the mouth.

The mention of Rossler's name was never more than a few words away from Corta's during the press coverage of her rehabilitation. When she was able to walk again, he was hailed as a miracle worker. Citizens across the nation called him a hero when Corta's personal Feed came back to the Net, streaming her workouts and combat training. And the word "Rossler" had echoed through the cacophony in the arena earlier that day at the emergency CookTalk, in which Cook announced Corta's surprise return to United America's Next Top Soldier. And he was more than pleased to accept the credit. It was, after all, his own simulation that had solved the puzzle. It was his hands that connected leads to neurocircuits and connected the nanomuscle tissue. His name now rang out across the entire nation.

A tone sounded. "Sir," J.A.Q.i announced, "It seems you have missed the fact that your name was just mentioned on NewsFeed."

"By whom?" Rossler asked.

"President Cook," J.A.Q.i replied.

"Shit...reopen NewsFeed. Turn the volume back up," Dr. Rossler ordered. "Replay from beginning of mention."

"...Not anymore, they're not," President Cook was saying through a camera drone Feed from the Oval Office.

"I am pleased to announce that Dr. Ben Rossler, the man who brought Corta back, is actively working on Mad Dog and Hax as we speak. The prognosis is good, and they will *both* be back in action by this evening."

"Wait, BOTH!?!" Rossler barked through his mask, his concentration finally fully snapped. In his panic, his hand jerked slightly, nicking the femoral artery in Mad Dog's right leg.

"Ah, shit…seal that," he commanded to a medical drone. It immediately shot out a cauterizing laser and sealed the wound. "J.A.Q.i, restart the Feed from the moment we turned it off."

Cook's Feed blinked out and the screen returned to Pat Daniels and Amanda Stokes staring into the camera as the the text crawl below them displayed in all caps "MARLOWE KANA - INNOCENT!"

"Well, she is *not* innocent," Amanda was saying. "She has killed over a hundred soldiers, and she made terroristic threats to me in my own apartment! She is responsible for the razing of the Subs! She incited a terrorist organization to rise up in Atlanta and break her out of prison! She–"

"–Just a second, Amanda," Pat interrupted, "Well, I just can't believe this. President of the United American State, Stephen Cook, is joining us now. Hello, Mr. President!"

"Greetings, Pat. Hello, Amanda," President Cook said. "I was just watching, and I had to stream in to say that Amanda, you are one hundred percent right."

"...I am?" Amanda asked, bewildered. "Wait... Yes, of course I am..."

"Yes, you are," President Cook agreed. "And to that end, Marlowe Kana has to be held accountable. She has to be held accountable for the hundreds of soldiers she slaughtered this evening after someone on her team hacked all of their weapons and left them defenseless!"

"Is that what happened?" Pat Daniel asked. "Because I've been told that–"

"That is indeed what happened, and it was unbecoming of a United American State Soldier."

"Well, she was never a UASA soldier, sir," Pat stated. "It didn't exist until a few hours ago–"

Cook ignored him. "More than that, she committed outright murder. She damaged and destroyed national property. She caused a disturbance and incited terrorism. All of the things Amanda Stokes just listed out. And the fact that she and her accomplices saw fit to fight us rather than work with us toward justice is a crime we cannot forgive. It's the crime of terrorism. So to that end, I am announcing here and now that Marlowe Kana is *still* wanted by the United American State Army, as are all of her accomplices."

"I agree!" Amanda Stokes chimed in..

"But, sir," Pat Daniels asked. "Imagen is still in charge of the courts. She was just pardoned."

"She was pardoned by a corporation's Board of Directors, in a court this administration and its Army does *not* recognize" President Cook responded. "The fact that Alan Davis and the rest of the Board decided to dismiss a felon they no longer have the resources to apprehend changes nothing. As the Commander in Chief of the United American State Army, I am now also the Executive Producer for "America's Next Top Soldier." It is my decision that Marlowe Kana is still the final challenge for the show, and that she and her accomplices are still terrorists. They must *all* still face justice. No one has provided any evidence that clears her father of the charge of orchestrating Marlowe's prison breakout, so he will remain in Terminus Citadel."

A smile suddenly crawled across the President's face. "I'll tell you what I'll do," he said. "If Marlowe is brave enough to come to Terminus Citadel and participate in the final round of 'Next Top Soldier' tonight, I'll release her father and drop all charges against him. And if she can beat Corta and her squad by Champion Rules - the old three-on-three squad setup, with the competitor striking the final blow - I will grant her a full, legally binding pardon. Hell, her and all of her friends!"

"Three-on-three Championship Rules?" Pat Daniels asked. "But Corta has been solo all year! No one has strategized for three-on-three since, well…since before Marlowe retired! She doesn't even have a squad. Who will serve with her?"

President Cook grinned boyishly, his trademark tell that there was something special coming. "Well, I was going to make it a surprise but, hey, why not make it an event! Corta will be joined by her former competitors, Henry "Mad Dog" Cain and Alexis "Hax" Curtis!"

"But sir, Mad Dog and Hax are both out of commission!"

"Not anymore they're not," President Cook answered. "I am pleased to announce that Dr. Ben Rossler, the man who brought Corta back—"

"Enough," Dr. Rossler said. J.A.Q.i terminated the playback. Rossler looked into Dr. Vessey's eyes as she peered at him in dismay over her surgical mask.

"We have a lot of work ahead of us," he said to his team. "Let's get back to it."

25. A Day In The Life Of: Ama Afua

Victor Smith-Afua and his wife, Angela Afua, had never been more proud. After weeks of hard work and dedication, their daughter Ama had just completed her first ever signature move and graduated from a Television Champion White Belt to the Intercontinental Championship Yellow Belt at Sensei Coach Steve's American Martial Arts Academy.

"Go, baby!" Angela called out from the stands amidst the polite clapping of the other parents. Ama, wearing a smile nearly as wide as the belt she had just been awarded, held her new rank proudly above her head. With spotlights illuminating her from above, she stared into the darkness of the crowd toward where her parents were sitting and beamed. She fastened the belt around her waist, the massive medallion looped on the front covering nearly her entire torso. As she marched purposefully over to Sensei Coach Steve and stood before him, she stared at Sensei Coach Steve's World Championship Black Belt with respectful longing. It had more than triple the number of diamonds, sapphires, and rubies embedded in the AMAA logo on the front, and shone with a mesmerizing luster in the overhead lights that illuminated the Ringjo. One day, she just knew it, she, too, would be a World Championship Black Belt holder.

The student and the sensei bowed to each other respectfully. Sensei Coach Steve then took his position in the center of the Ringjo as Ama took hers beside him. Together, the two bowed to the crowd. They turned and bowed to each other. The audience applauded slightly louder, but only as loud as bored parents waiting early in the morning for their children's turn in the spotlight possibly could.

Sensei Coach Steve held up to his mouth the ceremonial microphone, also adorned with the AMAA logo. "Ladies and gentlemen, I am pleased to introduce the newest Intercontinental Champion Yellow Belt in the American Martial Arts Association, Ama Afua! Ama, is there anything you want to say to the audience?" He leaned over and held the microphone in front of Ama's face, despite the fact that it was not actually necessary for anyone to hear her already J.A.Q.i-amplified voice.

"I want to thank my mom and my dad," Ama said. The two answered with cheers and clapping. Victor placed his fingers in his mouth and let loose an ear-piercing whistle of praise. "And I also want to thank my biggest inspiration and my hero, Marlowe Kana."

The room went silent for a moment. A sprinkling of claps could be heard from the left side of the auditorium from a few of the parents and children who happened to support MK.

Someone on the right side of the bleachers yelled out an emphatic "BOO!" A few grumbles emanated around.

"Hey!" Victor Smith-Afua called out from the stands. "Don't boo my daughter! Don't boo a *child*! That's just not right!"

"You oughta raise her better!" The boo-er replied from the darkness of the room.

"Who said that?" Victor demanded. "Show yourself!"

"Parents, let's settle down, please," Sensei Coach Steve urged nervously.

"I won't settle down!" Angela Afua stated, standing up next to her husband. "Someone just booed my little girl!"

"And that definitely wasn't right," Sensei Coach Steve said from the Ringjo. "But please, let's all just–"

"--He can't get away with that!" Victor interrupted in anger.

"Why not?" the boo-er yelled. "You get away with letting your daughter worship a traitor and a coward!" The voice grew closer as the stranger approached Afua's parents.

"J.A.Q.i, lights!" Sensei Coach Steve ordered.

The house lights rose around the small, hundred-person auditorium, revealing the several dozen parents whose children were testing for their belt upgrades that morning. One of those parents, a tall and thin man whose only hair was a scruffy growth on his pale white face, was standing at the center base of the bleacher array, pointing his finger at the Afuas, who stood confused in the middle of the stands.

"Mister Wallace, will you please take your seat?" Sensei Coach Steve asked sternly. "You know that this is inappropriate!"

"No, I will not!" Mr. Wallace said, turning to face the Ringjo. "You know what's inappropriate? Auggies! And their snobby attitude, and their support of that traitor Auggie coward, Marlowe Kana! And their damn kids, too!"

"That's my daughter you're talking about!" Victor Smith-Afua yelled as he took a step down the stairs to face Mr. Wallace. Angela grabbed him by the arm and held him back.

"And she's not a traitor!" A mother said from the middle as she stood to face Mr. Wallace. Another mother stood a few rows up and yelled, "And she's not a coward!"

"You all saw the President's challenge earlier," Mr. Wallace snapped back. "Marlowe's too scared to face Corta! She attacks the woman and then runs from her!" Mr. Wallace spat on the ground and barked, "Pathetic!"

"She's going to face Corta!" A father yelled from the left side of the bleachers! "She just responded!"

"Bullshit!" Mr. Wallace yelled.

"No, she just did," a mother from the left added. "She just announced it through MKFan_9999's Feed! And NewsFeed is re-broadcasting it now! Look!" She pointed to the screens along the far wall of the Ringjo, which were currently displaying footage of a shaky camera attempting to focus on Marlowe's face.

"J.A.Q.i, volume!" Sensei Coach Steve yelled.

Everyone in the Rinjo fell silent and turned to their right to face the screens. The video from the streamed Feed finally settled and focused in on Marlowe's face, beleaguered and blood-spattered. Just beneath her was a huge crawl reading, "Breaking News: MK Speaks!"

"Now?" Marlowe said to someone just beyond the camera.

"Not yet," a young girl's voice could be heard replying from off-screen. "Just a moment."

The audience remained reverently silent as they gazed upon the nation's most famous face. Marlowe stared distantly beyond the lens. She was exhausted, yet seemed energized, her eyes as calm but as stirring and dangerous as a riptide under a cresting wave. Seconds rolled by. "What's going on?" Marlowe asked past the camera to Nines.

"Just a moment, I'm getting it focused," Nines said with a snicker.

"You're streaming," Jen said in the distance behind Marlowe with a sigh. "She's fucking with you."

Nines' laughter pierced the tense air of the RInjo. Marlowe rolled her eyes, then looked directly into the lens. "People of the United American State," she said in a voice completely devoid of humor. "You've heard a lot about me the past few months. Not everything you've heard is true. Some of you believe my story, and some of you don't. Some of you think that I deserve to go to jail, and some of you don't. I don't care. I really, really don't. Believe me or don't. But none of you – not one of you hearing this right now – can possibly believe my father had anything to do with any of this."

The entire audience filling the Ringjo unanimously agreed with nods and a few audible yeses.

"I served Imagen's Military and Security Division for ten years with distinguished service. I've done some very questionable things, yes. And you've seen them all. So while I am completely innocent in this case, I can actually see why some of you wouldn't believe me. But my father served Imagen for twenty years, and his country for over fifty in total, beginning with the Marines before the war. He has never, in his entire career, done anything questionable. He is a hero. And you all know it."

The audience in the auditorium murmured in agreement. Love or hate Marlowe, they all worshipped General Ashish Kana. The nation had collectively wept the day he retired from MilSec due to his slow deterioration from Alzheimer's, one of the few diseases that remained incurable. And they had all cheered when Imagen refused his resignation and assigned him to honorary service as a Living Legend, a morale-builder whose continued service contributed to the country's esprit de corps.

Marlowe took a deep breath during her pause. "Therefore," she said into the lens, "I am accepting President Cook's challenge."

The left side of the auditorium cheered and applauded loudly. The middle section clapped in a seeming daze. The right side booed and jeered.

"You're WHAT!?!" The Judge's voice could be heard out of frame, before the palm of his hand covered the lens of the camera. A loud clanging could be heard before the stream ended.

"And there you have it," Pat Daniels said from behind his desk on-screen. "The official response by Marlowe Kana, leaked by the MKFan_9999 channel just moments ago—"

"Mute, J.A.Q.i!" Sensei Coach Steve said aloud. "Everyone, please! SIlence!" He begged the parents.

The chatter of the crowd quieted, but some parents weren't done making their point. "See?" The mother from the left responded. "If you had a Pod and HUD lenses, you'd have known that about Marlowe!"

"Well I ain't that privileged!" Mr. Wallace said.

"Anyone can get them!" The parent on the left responded. "If you can't afford the premium version, you just get the ad-supported model from Imagen–"

"Who can afford to buy all the crap they advertise?" another parent from the right yelled. "Not us! Only you privileged Auggie pricks can!"

"Watch your mouth, buddy!" a man in the front row said, standing up and facing Mr. Wallace. "Just cause we have Pods don't make us Auggies!"

"What's wrong with augmentations?" Someone queried angrily from the left side of the bleachers. "They're legal! What's the problem?"

"They're unnatural!" Mr. Wallace yelled. "Pods, limbs, eyeballs…it's not natural! None of it! You think that just 'cause you only have a Pod, that don't make you augmented? You rich people…you're all alike!"

"Hank, come on now!" Another parent said from the middle-right of the room. "This ain't the place to talk politics!"

"It is when *she* makes it so!" Hank Wallace said, pointing back at Ama in the Ringjo.

"She's a child, Hank!" another parent said, standing to face him. "This isn't right!"

"That child has been indoctrinated!" Mr. Wallace said. "Her parents up there…they try to fake like they're just like us, but they ain't! They're just as bad as the rich assholes down there!" He pointed down the bleacher row to the leftmost side. "They separate themselves from us week after week, sitting down there whispering into their Pods and shining their fancy limbs, while we try to tell our kids we're all equal…well we're not! Marlowe Kana ain't equal! She's been getting away with murder her whole life, only now she's getting punished for it, and we have little kids saying she's their hero? That bitch Auggie is a traitor! And so is anyone who supports her!" He pointed back to the Ringjo and added, "Even the kids!"

"You motherfucker!" Angela Afua screamed as she left her husband's side and flew down the bleacher stairs, crashing into Mr. Wallace and taking him to the floor. Her fist jackhammered into his face. Victor immediately plunged down and joined the three parents trying to pull Angela off of Hank Wallace. Another parent from the right side of the bleachers leapt in to defend Hank, while more parents from the more affluent left side of the bleachers sped in to help break up the fight. Within moments, there were twelve parents fighting with one another in a chaotic, messy brawl.

"Children, in the ring, now!" Sensei Coach Steve ordered. The eleven other children who had tested and won their Intercontinental Championship Yellow Belts all flooded into the ring and joined Ama and Sensei Coach Steve, watching in dazed confusion as their parents fought ringside. Once they were safely inside, Sensei Coach Steve ordered "J.A.Q.i, deploy the L.L.A.P.D."

"Little League Anti-Parent Defense deployed," J.A.Q.i announced. The KillJoy taser drones required by every youth sports organization by law flew out of their bays and arrayed themselves around the brawl. Streams of blue lightning flew from prods surrounding the drone. The wrestling parents fell one by one to the ground, writhing in agony as their bodies seized uncontrollably.

"I love that part," Johnny Wallace said to Ama Afua, who laughed in response.

26. Of Mice And Men

Marlowe was trying her best to pace the floor of the EV plant's frustratingly tiny workshop. Space was already at a premium with all the tools, equipment, and furniture littered around the room, and having eleven warm bodies standing around didn't help. Still, there was just enough runway for Marlowe to indulge her aimless, frustrated movement. And given the nature of the NewsFeed footage that everyone had watched on the trip back from Amanda's apartment, she had reason to be very frustrated indeed.

She took three steps toward where Seraph, Austin, Nines, Jen, and William stood, lined up along the back wall of the workshop. She then spun on her heel and caught a glimpse of Sully sitting near the doorway to the bedroom where William slept. She walked three more steps to where Angel, Poet, and Jacobs hunkered by the door. She spun again, avoiding eye contact with The Judge, who was surlily leaning against William's workbench.

"You said full operational command, remember?" Marlowe snapped at The Judge, continuing to awkwardly pace the floor three steps at a time.

"As I said in the Jumper on the way back here, this isn't an operation! This is a trap!" The Judge said emphatically, abandoning his typical aloofness.

"It's only a trap if you don't *know* about it!" Marlowe cried, pounding her fist. "I am NOT going to let them execute my father!"

"You'd rather they kill *you* instead?"

"Pssssh!" Marlowe said with a sneer. "Three-on-Three Championship Rules - I've done it three times before, I can do it again!"

"You are playing into his hand," The Judge replied. "The footage worked! Cook's scrambling! He can't win legitimacy without you by his side or behind bars - and he can't have either if you don't go when he says, where he says. We are *winning* here!"

"What exactly are we winning?" Marlowe barked as she stood fast and faced the Judge. "He still has my dad! We're still going to be hunted if we don't go! We're still going to be shot on sight, if they can get their guns to work... Hell, he even blamed us for that! He forgets to nationalize the 'arms' in our armed services and now, the nation thinks we're terrorists. We are fucked! We need to– wait, you know what? I'm tired of this shit. I'm going alone."

"Unacceptable," The Judge replied. "That's suicide."

"It's all my father has!" Marlowe yelled. "I am going to get him, with or without your help! And if your little team won't move out of the way, they'll be coming with me anyway…at least, parts of them will!"

"Me!" Jacobs piped up, raising his hand and taking a step forward from the door.

"NO!" The Judge ordered.

"Okay, guess I'm not…" Jacobs muttered.

"No one is!" The Judge ordered. "There are other forces in play right now making preparations. I have everything under control. We need to–"

"–Your plans suck," Marlowe interrupted, getting up in the Judge's face. "You act like you have this all under control, strategized to the nth degree…you don't. We did this your way and now, we're doing it *my* way." She lowered her finger and took a step back. Addressing the room, she added "This isn't a discussion. You can join me or you can fight me and I'll take you down along with the United American State Army, President Cook, whatever's left of Imagen, and anything else that stands in my goddamn way."

Marlowe turned and marched with righteous fury toward the door. Angel and Poet both took a step to the side.

"Stop her!" The Judge ordered.

Jacobs, ever the loyalist, stood and braced himself in front of the door. Marlowe ducked her shoulder and plowed into him, the way she had torn through defensive linemen back in her United American State Football playing days. Jacobs left his feet and flew backwards as Marlowe took the door off of the hinges with his back.

Jacobs's arms and legs flew every which way as he rode the door down the gravel walkway. Marlowe marched past him and took off toward the gate.

Jen tapped Nines on the shoulder. "Let's go," she muttered. Nines grabbed her Pod and followed Jen to the door.

"What, you're going to run with her all the way to the Terminus Citadel?" The Judge asked sarcastically.

"...Better than sitting around here with a bunch of fake revolutionaries," Jen said over her shoulder as she reached the doorway. She paused for a moment, and then turned and faced The Judge. "You know what I don't get?" She asked, her hand on her hip.

"A lot of things," The Judge said with the corner of his mouth turned up.

Jen ignored him. "You went through all that trouble to bust her out of prison and get her on your side... All that talk, all that effort... And you're just going to let her march herself alone to the one place she can actually do us all a lot of good?"

"It's not part of the plan," The Judge answered.

"*What* plan?!" Jen snapped. "Cook just undid everything we've worked for! Your entire plan was undone by a one-minute speech on NewsFeed! There *is* no plan! There's only Marlowe, us, my father, and an invitation by the President himself to free all of us! And you're just going to sit there smirking, as if you saw any of this coming?"

"There's a better way!" The Judge said, slamming his fist on the workshop table.

"What is it?" Jen asked. "Do you know? Right here, right now -- do you know what to do next?"

The Judge struggled for words.

"That's what I thought," Jen said, turning to leave. She was briefly blocked by Jacobs, who was rotating the soreness out of his shoulder and rubbing the spot on his chest where Marlowe's shoulder had rammed into him. The two made eye contact. "Move," Jen insisted.

Jacobs looked up at the Judge, who waved dismissively toward them. Jacobs stood to one side and let Jen pass. Nines fell in behind her, eyes glued to the Pod in her left hand, while she raised her right hand high, waving her middle finger around to everyone in the room.

"Damn it!" The Judge barked, stomping his boot into the wooden floor of the EV plant's work shed. He huffed through his nostrils and seethed.

William took a few steps toward the door and then paused and faced The Judge. "Her father is a hero," he said, "And so is she. We can do more good with her than without her."

The Judge slid his eyes toward William. He took a deep breath. The scowl left his face as he regained his composure. "I guess you're going with her, too, then?" He asked as he leaned back against the workshop table and folded his arms over his chest.

"Nope," William said as he reached the doorway. "I'm gonna get this door fixed. We still need a place to work, don't we?"

The Judge surveyed the room. Every eye was sullen and glued to The Judge, waiting to hear what the plan was going to be.

"Goddammit," The Judge said with a sigh, realizing there was only one real play. "Poet, go get Marlowe. Angel, get her attention."

"Yes, sir!" They both barked in unison. Poet led Angel out of the doorway and double-timed it to catch up to Marlowe. Angel turned and faced Marlowe's direction, raising her biohacked sniper rifle to her shoulder and peering down the scope. She found Marlowe in her crosshairs just as she was approaching the gate. A muffled report whistled from the barrel of the rifle as a round whipped its way toward Marlowe's feet. It caught the ground between her legs mid-stride.

Marlowe froze. She whipped her head around to find Angel lowering her rifle in the distance and Poet jogging up to meet her, arms waving over his head, signaling her to stop. Between the two, she saw Jen and Nines staring in disbelief at the scene unfolding before them.

She raised her hands to her mouth and yelled, "What now?!?" She waited patiently as Poet closed the distance as quickly as he could, reaching Marlowe only after a full-on sprint.

Out of breath and doubled over from his all-out effort, he huffed and said, "We... we're going... with you..."

"Oh, thank God," Marlowe said as her body slumped in relief. "Come on," she said, slapping Poet on the shoulder as she began trotting back to the shed. "We've got a lot of work to do."

Poet grimaced and groaned as he sucked for air from between his legs. Out of breath, he began trotting back to the shed behind Marlowe.

"What's going on?" Jen asked as they approached.

"He says we're all going to the Citadel," Marlowe said, pointing her thumb over her shoulder at Poet. "Not sure what happened after I left, but whatever it was--"

"Wow," Jen said. "It worked."

"What worked?" Marlowe asked.

"Calling that Judge guy on his shit," Nines said without breaking her gaze from her Pod. "I'm cutting a video of it now... But look at this! His face..." She held up the Pod and showed a clip of Jen reading The Judge the riot act. Jen, Poet, Angel, William, Sully...all of their faces showed up. But the Judge's face was a blurry mash, as was Austin's when it briefly appeared in the clip. "How the hell does he do that?!"

"His facial recognition is scrambled at the server level? And look, Austin's too!" Jen pointed out. "Jesus... I want that!"

"Me too!" Nines chirped in agreement. "That's *so* fucking cool!"

"Maybe that Austin guy did it?" Jen asked.

"Yeah," Nines said, "He's not as much of a noob as you are."

"...Says the girl who doesn't know how to do it either," Jen jibed. Nines sneered, and then went back to studying her Pod.

"Maybe you should just ask him?" Marlowe suggested as she started toward the door.

"No way!" Jen and Nines both said in unison.

Marlowe froze and looked back at them. They quickly glanced at each other. "A real hacker figures shit out on her own," Jen remarked.

"I bet I get it first!" Nines insisted as she tapped away at her Pod.

"Already on it," Jen insisted, flicking the air and sorting through scripts.

"...Good to see you two getting along," Marlowe said with a laugh as she made her way to the doorway that William was repairing. "Need a hand?" She asked him as she walked up.

"I got it," William said. "Broke at the frame, see? Hinges are still attached. A few screws and nails and it'll be back to keeping the draft out."

"Maybe some rebar? Or titanium?" Marlowe added with a smile.

"Wouldn't help," William replied. "I don't think there's much out there that's truly Marlowe-proof."

"Technically, I broke the door down," Jacobs said as he emerged outside through the doorway, followed by The Judge. "Nice takedown, by the way," he added.

"Don't ever get in my way again," Marlowe warned him, her smile souring. "And I assume you'll be my Hitter in the finals?"

"...Really?!?" Jacobs said, his excitement causing his voice to squeak.

"Oh God," Marlowe said, rolling her eyes, "I already regret that decision..." She turned her attention to Angel, who was examining the scope on her rifle. "And you?" Marlowe asked. "Want to be my Sniper?"

"I'd be honored," Angel replied quietly. "And it's not like anyone else here could do it."

Marlowe smirked and nodded knowingly. "And you, mister moustache...what's the deal? Why the change of heart?"

"You are right. I did promise you full operational control," The Judge said in reply. "I need Austin here, but the rest of the team is yours."

Sully hobbled toward the doorway with Seraph under his right arm and Austin under his left. The Judge and Poet took over helping Sully as he crossed the threshold on his one good leg. Everyone back together, the team stood outside of the EV plant's shed and looked at Marlowe.

"Well, now that we're all here," The Judge noted. "We have 12 hours until the 'Next Top Soldier' finale. What's the plan?"

Jen saw the look of disapproval on Marlowe's face as she raised her hand. "Don't even," Jen said defiantly. "He's my dad, too."

"And I'm not staying here with Judge Creepy McCreeper and that weird hacker noob, and those two boring old men," Nines added.

"Hey!" Sully said. "I'm not boring!"

"We are old, though," William said with a chuckle. "But you really should show some respect--"

"--Whatever," Nines said. "Besides, someone needs to cover your Feed side of things, just in case they try to screw you again. And footage from inside the Jumper will make me riiiiiich!"

Marlowe knew that Jen and Nines both had a point. And both had their uses.

Moreover, she didn't have the time or energy to fight them. "It's settled then," she said. "We dust off at eighteen-hundred. I suggest you all get some rest…and food? Do we have any food?"

"No one can show their faces," The Judge said. "And having anything delivered would be too risky."

"I can raid the vending machines at the plant," William said. "They have some decent Imagen InstaMeals in there. Some noodles, a really good mini pizza--"

"--Good, great, go do that," Marlowe said as she walked through the door leading to the bed William kept in the back room. "I'm crashing. Someone make sure I'm up by seventeen-thirty."

The team took Marlowe's cue, and everyone took up stations to prepare for the evening's festivities. William handed his powered drill to Poet and gave him a short rundown of what needed to be done to get the door back on its frame before heading to the main plant to deprive the vending machines of any sustenance he could find. Angel and Jacobs took up security posts; Angel double-timing it to the hilltop she had once perched on while Jacobs found a secluded spot near the gate and stayed low and alert. The Judge and Austin retreated to the makeshift computer lab in the back corner of the shed, while Seraph headed to the Jumper to make sure it was flight ready. Jen and Nines were busy surfing the Net for any and all information they could find on server-level face recognition defeats, and Sully took a seat just outside the door that Poet was now working on, pulled out a cigarette, and took the first drag he'd had in almost a day.

Marlowe laid face-up in William's bed. She finally felt fully like herself for the first time in months. There were less than ten hours before dust-off on the first major operation she'd commanded since before she left foreign service. This was no show; this was war. And she settled into her wartime training with ease. Her mind didn't want to be clear, but she was able to keep it from wandering too far from focusing on the fight ahead of her for the most part. She took a deep breath in through her nostrils. She held it for ten seconds, and then exhaled through her mouth. Again, she inhaled. She held the breath. She slowly exhaled. And again, and again. The mindful focus on her breathing forced her system to let go of any extraneous panic, overriding the impulse with the primal need to keep oxygen flowing.

Breathe in…one…two…three… on up to ten, she counted in her mind. And again.

"Marlowe?" a voice said somewhere in the distance.

Breathe in…one…two…

"Marlowe..." The voice said again, much closer and louder. It sounded like her sister. "It's time," the voice continued.

Marlowe blinked several times. "What time is it?"

"Five-thirty," Jen answered.

"...Jesus, that was fast," Marlowe said while sitting up and turning. She placed her feet on the floor, stood upright, and marched past Jen, patting her on the shoulder.

"Game time," Marlowe announced as she entered the main room of the shed. "Let's go."

*****

Seraph turned a quarter in the pilot's seat of the Jumper and looked back at the team in the cabin. "Ready for takeoff, ma'am," she said to Marlowe.

Marlowe looked up at her. The pilot she'd only just met had a disposition that she would know from anywhere. This woman had served at some point. She looked to Seraph's sister Angel, sitting beside her in the co-pilot's chair. Angel nodded at Marlowe, professional as ever. Jacobs' eyes were wide and his head was tilted forward like an excited puppy's. Poet's elbows were on his knees, chin resting on his thumbs as his fingers were clasped in front of his face in repose. Jen's leg bounced nervously as she flicked the air and scanned for alerts on her HUD, while

Nines' face was buried in the handheld Pod she'd clearly claimed as her own.

A calm washed over Marlowe. She sat up straight, resting her hands on her legs. The scowl that she'd worn for months fell from her face. Her eyes became steel. "Whether you're joining me on the battlefield tonight or not -- as of this moment, we are a team," she said in a commanding tone. "None of us have served together in any capacity, and some of us haven't served at all. But in the past twenty-four hours, everyone on this craft has proven their mettle and has my trust. I am honored you are joining me on this mission."

Nines looked up from her Pod. Jen's focus shifted from the readouts on her HUD to Marlowe. Jacobs and Poet both cracked slight smiles. Angel nodded, and Seraph sat silent, ready to fly.

"But if we are going to survive what's about to come, I am going to need your trust," Marlowe said. "We are flying into hostile territory and we are doing so blindly. This is not my first rodeo. And I don't care if this is your first time or your fiftieth. We take nothing for granted, and what I say, goes. I am no longer a major, but I *am* in command. I need every one of you to tell me you will do exactly what I tell you, without question, from this point forward."

"Yes, ma'am," Jacobs said first, sitting up straight and snapping a smart salute.

"Absolutely," Poet answered.

"Yes, ma'am," Seraph and Angel in unison.

Marlowe looked at Jen and Nines. "Yeah," Jen said, ducking her eyes.

"Jen?" Marlowe said. "You don't have to go."

Jen's face shot up. "I'm going!" Jen said, her eyes defiant.

"Then I need you to say it."

"...Yes, ma'am," Jen said quietly.

Marlowe turned her attention to Nines, who was recording the speech. Marlowe grimaced and furrowed her brow. Nines smiled and belted out an enthusiastic, "Yes, ma'am, Marlowe, ma'am!" the bow atop her head bobbing as she nodded her head with every syllable.

Marlowe smiled. "Last chance," she said, addressing everyone. "Anyone want out?"

The only thing that could be heard was the humming of the Jumper's magnetic drive and the whirring of the turbine engines.

Marlowe raised her hand up and signaled to Seraph.

"Aye, ma'am," Seraph replied as the engines whirred loudly. The Jumper lifted into the air, skirted the tree line, and bolted through the late evening sky toward Terminus Citadel.

Marlowe surveyed the team as they all sat silent in their seats. Jen was staring at the floor, her legs bouncing and shaking nervously.

Marlowe reached over and tapped Jen on the shoulder. Jen shot her head up, gasping in shock.

"You okay?" Marlowe asked, already knowing the answer.

"This is all my fault!" Jen whispered, a tear falling from her eyes. "I shouldn't have called MilSec. None of this would be happening if I hadn't told them how to find you. I put our father in prison and forced you to see Amanda and I am so, so sorry Marlowe--"

"--Cut it out," Marlowe insisted gently. Jen's lip quivered as she looked back at the floor.

Despite being in game-time mode, Marlowe knew she couldn't just leave things like this. For the last day, she had kept at bay thoughts about the fates of her Alzheimer's-stricken father, her sister... about her reunion with the woman who had broken her heart and ruined her life. As they flew over the still burning Subs, her thoughts glanced over the death of Jen's boyfriend Michael and the dozens of

Subs dwellers simply due to her proximity to them, not to mention the hundred soldiers by her own hand. One day, she'd have to face up to everything she'd done. That moment wasn't now; but in the midst of fatigue and starvation and withdrawal from AMP, Marlowe was barely winning the battle over her own mind. And she knew her sister was having far worse luck in that fight.

"Jen, look at me," Marlowe ordered.

Jen reluctantly looked at her sister, but refused to make eye contact.

"Imagen and Cook did this," Marlowe said. "They withheld the footage. They falsely convicted me. They made me some trophy for a game. They killed Michael and imprisoned our father, all to get at me. This was *them*, okay? Not you."

Jen shifted her eyes to meet Marlowe's. Tears streaked down, splattering gently onto her clothes.

"...And I'm going to make them pay," she added.

Jen smiled a very slight smile and it broke Marlowe's heart. It was the same smile when Marlowe had stood up for her in school, and the same smile when she was in court and the evidence that would have put her away for life for dealing drugs suddenly went missing.

Jen nudged the green canvas go-bag at her feet toward Marlowe. "You're going to need this, I think," she said.

"...Thanks," Marlowe said, reaching down to grab the bag. She rifled through it and grabbed a few Battery bars and an AMP inhaler. As before, she tore into the nutritional supplement bars and devoured them in a single gulp. She chased them down with a full inhale of AMP, shuddering and growling through her teeth.

"You going to take some with you?" Jen asked as she wiped away her tears with the sleeve of her shirt.

"Can't," Marlowe said as she exhaled, shivering. "Instant disqualification if I bring it on the field. Besides, we may need it for later."

Jen lowered her eyes again. Marlowe put her hand on her sister's shoulder and got her attention. "There will be a later, Jen," Marlowe insisted softly. "Trust me."

"Approaching Terminus Citadel now, ma'am," Seraph stated. "And it looks like we're being escorted in."

"Well, that's a damn sight better than being shot down," Marlowe said. She shook her head back and forth, loosening her neck. She cracked her knuckles, then pulled one elbow over her chest, followed by the other. "Here we go," she said, resolutely.

"Hell, yeah!" Jacobs shouted, sitting up and slapping his legs in excitement. "I've always wanted to be on 'Next Top Soldier'! Let's do this!"

"...Can you do that again?" Nines asked, pointing the Pod at Jacobs. "I missed it."

It took Jacobs three tries before Nines got a take to her satisfaction. And not a moment too soon as their Jumper descended and landed just outside the gates of the courtyard of Terminus Citadel, the makeshift battlefield for what was promising to be a "Next Top Soldier" finale for the ages.

27. Battle Royale

"You're *not* watching any more and that's final!" Brian Millar said curtly to his daughter.

Britany Millar unwound her arms from across her chest and flung them into the air, exasperated. "This is *so* not fair!" she protested. She turned to her other father and pleaded, "Dad, tell him this isn't fair!"

"Brian, honey, she's got a point," David Millar said. "This isn't just hero worship anymore. This is national news! *Real* news! And it's important!"

"And her yellow Intercontinental Belt test earlier this morning that she missed because she was glued to the Feeds? That wasn't important?" Brian asked testily. "And her sleep schedule? And her health? She's already missed a day of classes because of this, and now her entire weekend has to be consumed by it?"

A tone sounded. "Miss Britany? Sirs? The 'Next Top Soldier' finale is beginning…"

Britany Millar looked pleadingly at Brian, a fresh pool of tears welled up in her eyes, ready to spill over at any second. "Dad…please…"

Brian looked at David. His eyes were also pleading. "This is history, Brian," David said. "How would you like missing out on it?"

Brian took a deep breath. He had to admit, it was killing him at that very moment to not be glued to the screen watching the beginning of what had to be the most important historical event in his life. "Fine," Brian said, "But just this once—"

The clatter of shoes on tile echoed throughout the kitchen as Britany darted past her fathers and into the living room. "Main screen, J.A.Q.i!" she shouted. "Now!"

The full-wall screen in the living room flickered and the United America's "Next Top Soldier" logo appeared in mid-zoom, flying toward the viewer from a star-filled backdrop. The title logo slid down the screen to just above the ever-present NewsFeed crawl, which was required by law to stay on every single Feed display during times of national crisis. The deep-blue background speckled with white stars faded away to show two men, both in their late thirties, their perfectly manicured hair both the same faux shade of chocolate brown. Robert Roberts, WarFeed's color commentator, and Bob Smith, play-by-play announcer, smiled into the camera as they waited patiently for the United America's Next Top Soldier theme music to finish its trumpeting crescendo.

"It's an electric morning here at the Terminus Citadel!" Bob Smith said as the music faded into the background.

"This prison-made-foreign active duty training facility couldn't possibly be a more fitting location for what is sure to be the event of the century. I'm Bob Smith…"

"…And I'm Robert Roberts -- and let me tell you, Bob, I. Am. EXCITED." Robert pumped his fist emphatically with each word.

"I think we all are, Robert!" Bob agreed. "This is possibly the most important moment in our lifetimes -- maybe in our entire nation's history! Marlowe 'MK' Kana, the three-time 'Next Top Soldier' winner and hall-of-famer who has come out of retirement just for this match, versus Sergeant Sabrina 'Senche' Corta, a young and rising star in the MilSec ranks."

"Major," Robert corrected. "We have just learned that Corta is now an officer!"

"Interesting time for a promotion!" Bob mused.

"Or the perfect time," Robert replied. "Given Marlowe's rank when she was arrested, this makes them both majors -- and sets the stage for a *major* showdown!"

"And what a showdown it will be!" Bob observed. "There is some baaaad blood between these two. Let's get right to the introductions!!"

Both announcers turned and smiled into the camera as trumpets once again blared the intro music. Seconds went by as Bob and Robert continued staring into the camera, plastic grins stretched across their faces. Eventually, the music faded. "Well, it looks like we're having some trouble in the control booth," Robert said nervously. "With the short notice, there's been a lot of hasty scrambling to get -- what's that?" He asked, putting his finger to his ear. "We have it? Okay, folks, here we go! Once again, let's set the stage!"

The trumpets began playing again. Bob and Robert disappeared from view. Filling the screen was a United American State flag blowing majestically in the breeze, followed by footage of a now-famous black panther from the Indianapolis Zoo, ceremonially named Sabrina by Imagen to help bolster their new star's presence across the country. The background faded to black and the panther morphed into a human figure; Sabrina Corta filled the screen.

"Service. Dedication. Honor. These are the tenets of the United American State Army. And who better to represent them on the field of battle than rising star Major Sabrina 'Senche' Corta--"

"J.A.Q.i, fast forward!" Britany ordered.

A dim tone sounded. "I can't, Miss Britany. This is a live event."

"Mute it, then!" she barked. "I don't want to hear about this lying bitch!"

The audio from WarFeed was silenced just as Brian, now seated beside his daughter on the couch, reprimanded her sternly. "We don't talk that way in this house."

"Well, she is!" Britany insisted.

Brian looked to David for some backup. David shrugged. "I have to agree. Corta lied."

Britany smiled and widened her eyes innocently at Brian. Brian shot David a look . Then he considered the moment.

"Well, yeah…she kinda *is* a lying bitch, isn't she?" Brian admitted with a grin. "Okay, fine.. Just this once."

The three turned to look at the screen. In unison, they shouted...

*****

"Bitch!" Omar Rodriguez said to his best friend John via their shared chat channel.

"I'm not a bitch!" John snapped back. "The odds are terrible! I'm not betting!"

"Then admit that you know MK is going to win!"

"Not a chance!" John insisted. "Odds or no, you're insane if you think Marlowe wins this!"

"Dude, look at it!" Omar replied through a mouthful of partially chewed Imagen CheezRanch Triangles. "MK is pissed, Corta sucks...it's Marlowe all the way! In fact, I bet it's over in--" A tone sounded, interrupting him. "Ahh, shit man, hold on."

"Gabby again?" John asked, rolling his eyes. "Just block her ass, man. End this shit."

"Just...hold on, okay?" Omar said. "J.A.Q.i, switch to Gabby."

"Hey!" Gabby said perkily the second the chat connected. "I know you're about to watch 'Next Top Soldier' and all but I had to call real fast and tell you how much I love you!"

"Gabby," Omar said with a sigh. "It's over. I broke up with you hours ago. You've got to stop calling."

"But...this is a mistake!" Gabby replied, holding back tears. "Who else is going to call you and let you know they love you every morning? Huh? Who else?"

"Goodbye, Gabby," Omar said, terminating the call. The chat window closed, and John's face came back into view. "J.A.Q.i, block Gabby," Omar added.

"Finally!" John said, overhearing Omar's order. "It's about time you got rid of her for good, man. And just in time to see your hero's entrance!"

Omar shifted his focus from John's window to WarFeed. A smiling Bob Smith and a grinning Robert Roberts were mid-sentence, introducing the competitors.

"Marlowe Kana and her squad are standing in the center of the Terminus Citadel courtyard," Bob Smith said. "These two new faces Marlowe has with her are unknown quantities. No one knows anything about former Private First Class Robert Jacobs and former Sergeant Mila "Angel" Pavil, except that they were part of this enigmatic crew that broke Marlowe out of the prison transport last night. But what is known is just how dominant Marlowe Kana has always been in the 'Next Top Soldier' finale, regardless of who is by her side. Isn't that right, Robert?"

"Indeed, Bob," Robert replied, "The contest is five years old, and she's been Champion for three of them, opting to retire in 2095, thus vacating the title. But she's back, and if she wins tonight, a fourth belt is hers!"

"And what an interesting place for the finale to take place, isn't that right, Robert?" Bob asked.

"It sure is, Bob," Robert Roberts replied. "I suppose with her father being released here, it makes sense. At least he gets to sit ringside to watch his daughter fight for his honor!"

"These guys suck," Omar said to his friend John, a half-chewed CheezRanch Triangle falling from his mouth. He picked it off his shirt and stuffed the soggy morsel back into his gaping maw.

"Yeah, I miss Joe and Joseph," John said in agreement. "They were funny. These guys are just too... announcer-y."

"Shh!" Omar shushed. "They're showing the battleground!"

"The Terminus Citadel courtyard is convenient in more than one way as a battleground," Bob was saying. "Most of the fixtures for a Finals Battleground are already here — no need for set construction. We have towers for the Snipers, and fenced off areas that can serve as the Hitter's Bullpen — and speaking of Hitters, here she is now!" Bob announced as Marlowe and Corta approached a floating drone in the dead center of the courtyard. Major Sabrina Corta is making her entrance, and look at that -- she's got Alexis 'Hax' Curtis and...is that Mad Dog?!"

"He's hardly recognizable!" Robert Roberts crowed. "He's got a full body replacement!"

"Should make him a great hitter!" Bob said. "And with both finalists and their squads approaching the referee drone, the pre-fight ceremonies are about to begin! Both contestants approach the announcement drone for introductions and--HOLY MOLY!"

The camera shook trying to keep up with the speed of Marlowe's fist as she slammed it square into Corta's chestplate. The newly minted major went airborne, flying ass-first into the iron gate guarding the main entrance doorway of the Terminus Citadel.

"Oooooh and Marlowe strikes first!" Bob Smith announced. "It's always been in the rules that the finals start the second both competitors step foot on the field, but never before has anyone broken the unspoken rule of striking before the handshake! This is quite the statement from Marlowe Kana — she came to play, and she came to *win*!"

"SEE!" Omar Rodriguez yelled triumphantly at John. "I told you Marlowe's got this!"

*****

"Completely unsportsmanlike!" A gym member unknown to Glen cried out.

Glen Russel knew that manspreading on a piece of equipment while there were others waiting was a violation of gym etiquette, but no one was actually asking if he was done. The entire gym had their eyes glued to the screens hanging from the ceilings in front of the CardioBar.

Glen wasn't in a hurry to continue his workout anyway. His arms were still sore from the hundred pushups he had to do the night before, after foolishly betting that Henry "Mad Dog" Cain would be able to take Marlowe Kana in. It was surprising, then, for him to see Mad Dog on the field of battle with Corta, especially after seeing the footage of his broken body being carried to the hospital. Glen remembered his own long path to recovery after losing his leg...months of agonizing frustration as his body had to learn to control the neural interfaces for his augmented leg. How one man could take that much damage and survive was surprising; how he could possibly get back on the field so quickly was nothing short of miraculous.

Watching as Mad Dog strutted into the courtyard with Corta had been immeasurably inspiring to Glen. But watching Hax and Angel suddenly realizing that the games had started and they needed to get to their battlestations tout suite...well, that had made everyone in the gym laugh.

Hax and Angel both sprinted to equidistant watchtowers along the outer wall of the Terminus Citadel. Mad Dog and Jacobs trotted to the makeshift "Hitters Boxes" that were constructed in lieu of the standard plexiglass enclosures where the squad members waited for the appropriate time to assist.

"Well, since we're already started, I guess we'll go through the rules quickly!" Bob Smith chirped up. "It's been a few years since we've had these rules, so as a reminder for the citizens watching, unlike the solo rules the last two years, in three-on-three Champion Rules matches, each contestant has two Squad Assists they can use: the Sniper and the Hitter."

"That's right, Bob," Robert said. "Now, Snipers only have one tranquilizer round each, and they can only fire on the minute; that is, at 59 seconds, they can take aim, but they can only fire once that clock rolls over to the double-zeros."

"Indeed, Robert," Bob said, taking over. "So their decision on when to fire is critical — do they take their shot early on, and risk having a fresh and rested soldier dodge their fire, or wait until the contestant is worn down, but risk letting the opposing sniper take the more helpful, early shot? It's a critical decision, to be sure."

"It's never happened in 'Next Top Soldier' finale history, but I wouldn't be surprised if we heard a shot at the first minute, Bob!" Robert said. "Especially if Hax chooses to use the technovirus that he used earlier against Marlowe Kana."

"No doubt it was super effective, Robert," Bob said. "It would be advantageous to infect her early on, but that also ruins any chance of a rescue shot later if he misses!"

"We're at twenty seconds and no sign of Corta," Robert said. "We may not even get the chance for Snipers or Hitters to come into play, Bob!"

"See?" The new gym-goer barked, tearing everyone's gaze away from the gym's screens. "This is why auggies can't be trusted!"

"Aren't you rooting for Corta?" Glen asked the new guy.

"Well, yeah. Duh," he answered.

"Corta's augmented. So are Mad Dog and Hax."

"Well, they're different!" The new gym member insisted. "They're patriots. They didn't cheat."

"Corta was literally caught lying about attacking Marlowe first not two hours ago by Amanda Stokes," Glen retorted. "How does that make her a patri--whoa!" Glen ducked the sudden punch thrown by the guy and tumbled off of the gym equipment he was sitting on.

"Gentlemen!" a burly bodybuilder said, stepping between them. "Let's just chill and watch the fight? All right?"

"Yeah, fine," the new member said. "I don't want to talk to this fucking auggie anymore, anyway!"

The bodybuilder extended his hand and helped Glen to his feet. "Don't listen to him," he said. "Tensions are high."

"Yeah, I'll say," Glen said, rubbing his bottom.

"What a night!" Bob called out on-screen. "Not even thirty seconds in, and it's already an incredible, *incredible* night!"

*****

"What's so incredible? What did I miss?!" Angela Tuffner asked her husband Matt as she emerged from the bedroom. "Oh my God, MK is back on UATS? And she's fighting Corta!? Dammit, why didn't you wake me?!"

"You were exhausted. You needed sleep," Matthew replied.

"I didn't need twelve hours of sleep!" Angela insisted.

"Yes you did," he replied. "But hey -- I did make you this." He slid a tumbler full of coffee her way.

Angela smiled. Ten years of marriage, and he was still as thoughtful as he was from the beginning. "Scooch," she said, squeezing next to him on the couch. "What happened?"

"Marlowe knocked Corta through the gate like thirty seconds ago," Matthew replied as the fight clock on-screen ticked over to 0:31. "If she's not back in twenty-nine seconds, the fight is over."

"Wow, one-second knockout?" Angela asked, taking a sip from her coffee.

"I kinda hope it happens!" Matthew said. "What a crazy couple days it's been...Marlowe breaks out of prison, proves her own innocence, then comes back to 'Next Top Soldier' and wins her fourth title in *one* second?"

"Well, I kinda hope it doesn't!" Angela said. "I wanna see a fight! Corta better get back in there!"

"We are fifty seconds in," Robert was stating on-screen. "Only ten seconds left for Corta to get back into play, or she'll be disqual--Wait, there she is!"

The camera drone zoomed in on the destroyed gateway of the Terminus Citadel to show Major Sabrina Corta stomping her way through the wreckage and out of the building. "She's in play!" Bob Smith announced, "No disqualification! But will we hear Sniper fire this first minute?"

"It's never happened before," Robert Roberts noted, "As Snipers are usually backup--"

A loud *CRACK*! pierced the audio of the Feed, interrupting Robert.

"Sniper fire on the first minute!" Bob shouted. "I can't believe it! A first! Who's down? Who fired?" The camera drone zoomed out to show Corta still approaching

Marlowe, who stood ready to face her. "Neither contestant is down, but someone fired — wait! Look there!"

One of the Feeds zoomed in on the tower on Corta's side of the courtyard to find a slumped and snoozing Hax, leaning over the edge of the tower, his rifle teetering precariously on the edge of the wall, an inch away from a fifty-foot fall.

"Holy moly!" Robert shouted. "Angel has taken out Hax!"

"Oh my god!" Angela said, spilling her coffee as she jumped up in shock. Glancing over at her husband, she noticed that most of her spilled coffee had landed in his lap. "Oh no, oh Matt...I am so sorry!"

"Screw it! It'll wash out," Matthew replied, wincing slightly. "This is history!"

*****

"I don't care how historic this is," Matthew Swift's father hollered from the J.A.Q.i -piloted limousine. "You're in a lot of trouble!"

"I mean, the *subs*?" Matthew's mother asked in frank dismay. "Matthew, really!"

Matthew sighed and kept his focus on the screen in the center of the limo. "Are you two seriously not watching this?" Matthew asked. "I'll still be in trouble when I get home. But this is happening *now*! Real history, right in front of us!"

"Great!" His father barked. "You watch history while we watch your future slipping away!"

"I wasn't even charged!" Matthew replied. "This won't impact a thing!"

"But what about the precedent it sets?" His mother asked. "You want us to not care if you go cavorting with drug dealers and prostitutes and God knows what else is down there?"

"I want you to trust me when I tell you, I was just — Holy shit!" Matthew yelled. "Corta's got Marlowe in a headlock!"

His parents scowled, yet Matthew noticed they couldn't help but glance over at the screen themselves.

"Corta has Marlowe around the head, and is slamming her fist right into her face!" Bob was saying on-screen.

"Marlowe's in trouble!" Robert added. "She's got Corta around the waist -- she's going for a suplex! Corta has let go of her head and is grabbing at Marlowe's hands…and she's free! Corta has broken free!"

Marlowe and Corta stumble a few steps away from one another. Marlowe's nose dripped blood and her eye was swollen; Corta's lip was split and gushing blood. Corta flashed a bloody grin at Marlowe. Marlowe wiped her nose with her hand and looked at the blood on her fingertips. She smeared it across her chest, leaving a crimson stripe across her white tank top. She pointed at Corta and then dramatically gave her a thumbs-down.

"The guts these two soldiers are displaying...it's unbelievable!" Bob shouted. "This is one hell of a fight!"

"Look at MK, Bob!" Robert crowed. "A dozen blows to the face, busted nose, swollen eye, and she's not even phased!"

"And we're nearing the two-minute mark, in which those mighty, mighty Hitters are allowed to assist for thirty seconds!" Bob said.

"Well, Bob, I'm just now hearing from the booth that Mad Dog's brain has been wired into that new body! In fact, it's the only part of his anatomy that's actually his own! And from the looks of it, it seems that in his state after surgery, he's quite unstable!"

"Very dangerous strategy, using him like this!" Bob noted. "But, completely within the rules!"

"We know how hard Mad Dog can hit, Bob," Robert said. "But this person on Marlowe's side — he's a relatively unknown entity. All we know is that he was part of the gang that broke Marlowe out last night."

A window appeared on the screen, showing a frozen frame from the drone footage of the prison break the night before with Jacobs grinning and flipping off the camera. "That's former Private First Class Robert Jacobs," Bob said. "He does look scrappy, doesn't he, Robert?"

"He sure does," Robert agreed. "But how can he possibly take on a now fully augmented Mad Dog?"

"And there's the buzzer for the two-minute mark!" Bob called as the doors to the Hitters' Boxes opened and Mad Dog and Jacobs rushed the field. "Look at this newcomer go! Cain seems to be headed for Marlowe and Corta. Jacobs doesn't seem to be even remotely worried as he's sprinting headlong right toward Cain!"

"Well, judging by the events of last night, he has to know that Mad Dog's only desire is to crush Marlowe Kana," Robert noted. "He's got revenge on his mind, and a brand new shiny body with which to exact it!"

"But how on earth will Jacobs handle all that titanium and steel?" Bob asked.

Jacobs leaped off his feet as he neared Mad Dog, who was mid-stride, heading toward the middle of the field where Corta and Marlowe were circling each other. Jacobs extended his arms and attempted to wrap them around Cain in a furious, open-field tackle. However, Cain, in his new, fully robotic body, barely stumbled as Jacobs slammed shoulder-first into him. Jacobs slid down Mad Dog's leg and collapsed on the field, dizzy from the impact.

"...Not very well at all, Bob," Robert stated. "Cain just stood up to Jacobs' tackle like a brick wall!"

"Well, Jacobs is not giving up!" Robert said. "He's back on his feet...he's rushing toward Cain! He's got his fist cocked...hooo boy! That had to hurt!"

On-screen, Jacobs's face crumpled and his teeth were bared in pain as he grabbed his now-mangled right hand. "It doesn't look like Marlowe's Hitter is doing much good hitting, as Cain is undeterred and making his way over to Marlowe!" Bob said with a chuckle.

Jacobs shook his head and narrowed his eyes. He got up and sprinted after Cain. "Look at that," Robert called. "He's jumped on Cain's back!"

"But it hasn't slowed him down at all as he's just reached Marlowe!!" Bob reported. "Cain is rearing back, preparing to strike...and Jacobs has just grabbed Mad Dog's arm and is hanging from it like a monkey!"

Cain attempted to punch toward Marlowe, but the swinging weight that was Jacobs' body kept his fist from connecting. Marlowe leaped nimbly out of the way, then darted to the other side of Mad Dog and Jacobs, forcing Cain to turn to face her.

"His movements seem slow and clunky," Bob said.

"One has to wonder just how much of Mad Dog's brain is in that body," Roberts added. "He seems to be on autopilot!"

The fight clock struck two minutes and twenty seconds. A loud buzzer sounded in the distance.

"Well, he missed his one shot, thanks to Jacobs," Bob answered. "We are nearing the two minute and thirty-second mark, and the buzzer has just sounded for the Hitters to clear the field."

"Jacobs has dropped from Mad Dog's arm, and is running as fast as he can back to his box," Robert said. "Now Mad Dog is headed back and…wait, he's stopped. He's turning around…he's headed back to Marlowe Kana!"

"It seems Mad Dog is refusing to leave the field!" Bob yelled. "Corta is yelling at him to leave… If he isn't off the field in seven seconds, Corta is disqualified!"

"Corta is furious! She's screaming at him to…wait, what's this? Corta is leaping into the air and...OH MY GOD! Sabrina Corta has just attacked her own Hitter! She has kicked Mad Dog back into the Hitter's Box!"

Just then, a tone sounded. "Sir, Ma'am, Matthew," J.A.Q.i announced calmly. "We have arrived at your condo--"

"Quiet!" Matthew's mother yelled.

Both Matthew's and his father's heads shot up as they looked at the mother in complete surprise. She scowled disapprovingly, then returned her attention to the screen just in time to see Marlowe wrapping her arms around Corta's waist.

"Marlowe's got Corta from behind!" Bob screamed. "She's going again for the...SUPLEX! YES! She nails it! She's just slammed Corta head-over-heels into the turf! Surely that has to have--NO! Corta's up! My word! She's not even phased!"

"Man, what a fight!" Matthew's father cheered from the back seat of the limo. His tone changed and became more dour as he suddenly remembered why he was in the back of his family limo hovering outside of his condominium in downtown Atlanta having just picked up his son from the MilSec-turned-UASA precinct. "...Don't think that this fight has gotten you out of trouble," he said grimly to his son, furrowing his eyebrows.

"I know," Matthew replied, his smile sliding off his face as he returned his attention to the fight.

"And we're now at three minutes. With Angel having taken her shot and Hax down as a result, there'll be no assistance for either side," Bob was saying on-screen.

"That's right, Bob," Robert said, "And Jacobs and Mad Dog still have a minute left before they can assist again."

"It looks like they'll get that chance, and possibly a few more, Robert!" Bob said cheerfully. "This fight shows no signs of stopping! Look, Marlowe is picking Corta up for a bodyslam! She has Corta overhead...wow! Corta has wriggled free! She's behind MK, and has her around the waist...Is it a suplex? Wait, no, she's just taken Marlowe down with a forward sweep!"

"Corta is going for the back mount...she's pushing Marlowe's face into the grass! She's rearing back, going for the knockout...Marlowe is standing up! Corta is holding on for dear life, wrapping her arms around Marlowe's neck!"

"Corta is choking Marlowe out!" Bob yelled. "Marlowe is slumping! But the question is, is this a fake-out?"

"It's definitely a fake-out," Matthew's mother murmured.

Matthew and his father looked over at his mother again.

"She did that in season two," she explained with a slight smile, eyes never leaving the screen.

*****

"I don't know," Regina Todd said as she took another sip of coffee from the booth she shared with her brother Reginald, her friend Tad, and their server friend Marc Winter. "She looks like she's going out."

"Nah," Marc Winter said. "MK is faking it. Corta should know that."

"How do you know?" Reginald asked. "Her eyes are rolling back. She's blacking out."

"I'm a student of history," Marc replied. "I've seen every single one of Marlowe's fights and missions. I've seen her play opossum before."

"...What's a opossum?" Tad asked.

"It's *an* opossum," Marc replied with a chuckle. "They used to be, like, really big rats. They ate garbage and dog food off people's porches."

"Wait, people *really* used to have dogs?" Tad asked. "I thought that was just an urban legend."

"...And what's a rat?" Regina asked.

"...Watch the fight," Marc said, taking a sip from his own coffee cup.

"...We are coming up on the four-minute mark, Bob," Robert announced. "But with both snipers down, it'll be up to the Hitters to provide any assistance-- wait, what's this?"

"I can't believe it, Robert!" Bob yelled. "Hax is back! Look at that, he's rising to his feet!"

"Yes, Bob! In a finals where the unexpected has become the norm, Hax has emerged from the tranquilized haze imposed by the opposing Sniper's dart and is now reaching for his rifle!"

"It looks like it's time for the Imagen CheezRanch Triangle TRIGGERCAM!" Bob cheered, as a yellow-and-white dotted triangle with the Imagen logo scrawled on top in faux-cursive appeared in the corner of the screen showing Feed footage from directly down the barrel of Hax's rifle.

"And there's the shot!" Robert said. The TRIGGERCAM Feed footage shook as Hax pulled the trigger on his rifle. Just as he did, the doors to the Hitters' Boxes on either side of the courtyard swung open. Marlowe knew that time was short. She posted her leg and wrapped her arms around Corta, attempting to roll her on top and into the path of the nanovirus dart. Corta's one arm flailed, trying to keep Marlowe from rolling her over, but it was useless. Marlowe twisted Corta over easily, but not quickly enough. The TRIGGERCAM! feed closed in on Marlowe's shoulder.

Just then, a blur streaked across the TRIGGERCAM! feed. The dart made impact and the screen went black. The Feed switched back to the aerial drone's camera, which showed Corta on top of Marlowe and just as Jacobs landed heavily in the grass beside them in the courtyard, a dart protruding from his shoulder.

"I did NOT see that coming!!!" Robert Roberts shrieked. "Jacobs has leapt nearly ten yards from the Hitter's Box and intercepted Hax's dart! My word! Yet another first in a 'Next Top Soldier' finale that is destined for the history books!"

"But that takes him out of play and leaves Marlowe alone against Corta and Cain -- And here comes Mad Dog!" Bob shouted. "He's just approached Marlowe's side of the field! Corta is releasing Marlowe and giving him an opening! He's sure to crush— wait a minute, he's stopped! What's he doing?"

"He's just…standing there!" Robert Roberts observed as Mad Dog's forward movement ceased and his body began shaking erratically.

"He's very jittery, Robert," Bob added. "He seems to be unsure of what to do!"

"He's raising his fist!" Robert announced. "He's rearing back...Corta has stepped away, and Marlowe is scrambling to get out of the way! He's swinging -- oh my! He just grabbed his own fist and intercepted himself! He's...he's spinning!"

"What on earth is going on!?" Bob cried. "Mad Dog just intercepted his own punch and is pirouetting around like a ballet dancer! This is just...I've never seen anything like it!"

"Corta's beside herself!" Robert observed. "She's ordering Cain to smash Marlowe, who is now on her feet and circling! Why isn't Mad Dog striking? Wait, Bob!" Robert interrupted himself, "I'm just now hearing this from the booth, and oh my lord, citizens of the United American State, I cannot believe this but someone is *hacking* Mad Dog!"

"That's right, someone has taken control of Henry 'Mad Dog' Cain!" Bob explained. "It just keeps getting crazier here at the 'Next Top Soldier' finale! Marlowe is rushing Corta in the confusion and has taken her down! She's got the mount...Mad Dog is raising his left fist this time...haha, I cannot believe this! He just intercepted his own punch again! There he goes, spinning around! Who is doing... Wait, look at the Feed, Robert!"

One of the drones covering the fight suddenly zoomed in on Jen and Nines from just outside the front gate of the courtyard. Nines was staring into her Pod screen and Jen was waving her hands in the air, tapping commands on an invisible interface as she fired off script after script. Both of their faces were blurred from view for the audience at home, both having figured out the IdentServer hack by finally teaming up (and with a little help from Austin). Nines tapped Jen's arm and showed her the Pod in her hand. Both Jen and Nines looked up at the drone broadcasting them. Jen waved at the camera; Nines flipped her middle finger at the audience watching.

"Well, isn't that a fine how-do-you-do, Robert!" Bob said. "Nice way to say hello to the entire nation! We can't see their faces, but we can certainly see that middle finger from Marlowe's hacking team!"

"Yet another first in 'Next Top Soldier' history!" Robert observed. "We're being told that, despite this being highly unorthodox, there is no rule preventing this!"

"In fact, the rules specifically say that hacking is a valid tactic against augmented soldiers!" Bob added. "We saw it last night when Hax controlled Marlowe, and now again in these finals!

"I guess all's fair in love and war, Bob!" Robert opined.

"Except pointing a gun at grafitti artists," Tad muttered from his side of the table at the Waffle House.

"You're gonna have to get used to that," Marc Winter commented as he sipped again from his cup of coffee.

"Why's that?" Regina asked, seated next to her brother Reginald. "You know Marlowe's gonna win... Then it all goes back to normal, right?"

"Ain't nothing normal about any of this," Marc replied. "MK's court martial, the suppressed evidence, the jailbreak... Now we have an emergency 'Next Top Soldier' finale, where one of the contestants is pretty much a full robot being remote controlled, and the Subs are nothing but ashes... I have a feeling, ain't nothing going to ever be the same."

"Is this how it was before...you know, the war?" Reginald asked Marc.

Marc shifted in his seat. He cleared his throat and gestured his coffee mug toward the monitor on the wall across from their table. "Watch the fight," he said curtly.

*****

Ama Afua sat in the United American State Army precinct's uncomfortable plastic chair in her martial arts gi, her brand-new yellow Intercontinental Champion belt laid across her lap. Her father and mother sat subdued on either side of her, pointedly not making eye contact with the rabble-rousing Mr. Wallace. Sensei Coach Steve sat at the desk of the private assigned to take his statement as to why his American Martial Arts studio had to deploy the L.L.A.P.D. system. It was standard procedure whenever the parent determent systems were used. And it happened nearly every week. The Afuas, the Wallaces, and Sensei Coach Steve were all pretty used to being at the precinct at this point.

This time, however, no one was giving a statement. No one was fighting. No processing was taking place. Ama's legs had stopped swinging as they dangled from the chair. The private's pen had long since fallen from his hand. Ama's mother Angela had dropped the ice pack she held to her eye, and her father Victor had stopped re-wrapping his wrist bandage. Sensei Coach Steve and the private were both staring at the screen - a half-written statement lay in front of them on the desk.

"That's BULLSHIT!" Wallace suddenly barked from across the waiting room. "MK is cheating!"

The room immediately sounded like someone was letting all of the air out of it, as a chorus of "SHHHHs!" erupted.

"Well, she is!" Wallace insisted. "Look--"

"Shut up!" the duty sergeant ordered.

Mr. Wallace started to snap back at the soldier, but then remembered he was in handcuffs. He sullenly returned his attention back to the screens situated around the precinct, just in time to watch as Mad Dog began jerking and twitching.

"Henry 'Mad Dog' Cain seems to be completely unable to control himself," Roberts was announcing. "He keeps raising his right fist to punch, but then pulls it down with his own left hand!"

"In what is undoubtedly the most incredible 'Next Top Soldier' finale we've ever seen, *this* is truly a unique event," Bob Smith hooted. "We have remote control of an augmented soldier passing between opposing teams! This is just something, isn't it, Robert? And what's this…it looks like Mad Dog's about to strike! His fist is raised -- but who is he going to attack? Who's got control of his body?"

Mad Dog stood with his fist reared back as Marlowe and Corta both tussled on the ground, struggling to stand. With a loud yell, he swung his fist forward and around, and struck himself squarely in the face.

"Oh my God!" Wallace yelled in the precinct. "That's illegal! That's so illeg--"

A blue arc of electricity flew from a terminal in the ceiling, shocking Wallace. "Enough," the sergeant said, removing his finger from a button embedded on his desk.

"Mad Dog has just knocked himself out!" Roberts announced. "He's falling…oh my God, he's fallen on Major Corta! He's pinned her leg! She's stuck!"

"That is a terrible angle for her leg to be in!" Bob Smith observed with unholy glee. "Mad Dog's body has landed sideways on Corta's knee and she is screaming in bloody agony! I don't know how she's going to get free!"

"Well, if Cain's not off the field in seven seconds, it won't matter!" Robert said. "Marlowe has only a few seconds to strike the final blow before Mad Dog's presence on the field disqualifies Corta, and leaves the championship in limbo!"

"And if that happens, Bob, it's unclear if Marlowe will still be pardoned!" Robert added. "A disqualification for Corta is NOT a victory for Marlowe, as she well knows! All the chips are on the table -- and HERE SHE COMES! MK is on her feet and stumbling toward her trapped opponent, she's going to end this...wait!"

Everybody in the precinct watched in awe as Marlowe stopped just in front of the Mad Dog and Corta sandwich. She reached down and wrapped her hands around Cain's augmented left ankle.

"What is this!" Roberts shrieked. "She's grabbing Mad Dog by the leg! She's spinning him -- Bob, she's ejecting Mad Dog!"

Marlowe spun around and around, swinging Mad Dog's metallic body in a wide arc before letting go and sending him sailing over the outside wall of the Terminus Citadel.

"I can't believe it!" Roberts yelled. "MK isn't going for the easy kill -- she's just thrown Mad Dog out of the ring!" A window appeared with the feed from a camera drone following Mad Dog's trajectory over the wall before he collided with the ground outside the Citadel.

"She doesn't want an asterisk on this victory, Robert," Bob opined. "She wants the nation to know that, if she wins, it'll be fair and square!"

"She's stepping back," Robert said. "I think she's setting up for…yes! It's her signature move! Corta's rising on her good leg…Marlowe is running…she's in the air! Her fist is back! Bob, It's an MK Ultra!"

Marlowe's fist connected with Corta's chest, sending her off her feet once again and flying across the Terminus Citadel courtyard. Corta's limp body bounced off of the turf once, then twice, and then a third time. The viewers in the precinct waiting room, and across the entire nation, joined Bob and Robert as they held their collective breaths while watching Corta skid face-down across the grass, finally coming to a halt near the wall on the east side of the courtyard.

"My GOD!" Bob Smith shrieked. "What a thunderous blow! No one has ever gotten up from an MK Ultra! Corta is out, folks! Corta is...wait, no...she's stirring! She's trying to get up!"

"I don't know how on earth she survived that punch," Roberts said, stunned. "And I can't believe she's trying to get up!"

"And look at Marlowe Kana's face," Bob observed. "She's as shocked as we are! She was certain that was it. She looks completely spent as she heads toward Corta to finish the job!"

"She's taking her time with it, Bob," Roberts observed. "She's exhausted, but my word, look at the swagger as she walks over to Corta."

"MK is just incredible," Bob noted. "After escaping prison, evading capture, taking out Mad Dog, Hax, and over a hundred soldiers, and then fighting a highly trained and newly augmented Sabrina Corta, she still has the pure grit to march across this field and get the job done. That's sheer will on display, right there."

"That's the march of a true warrior, Bob."

"A soon to be four-time champion, Robert."

"But wait! Corta's rising to her knees!" Robert yelled. "She's not going to stay down!"

"These two soldiers are just incredible," Bob observed. "This is the greatest display of heart I've ever seen on the battlefield. Sabrina Corta: fighting for her place alongside the champions of history. Marlowe Kana: fighting for her freedom. The stakes are high, and the word 'quit' isn't in either of their vocabularies and...OH MY GOD, Corta is up! Sabrina Corta has just stood up after an MK Ultra!"

"Corta is up!" Robert said. "Marlowe is picking up her pace! Corta is turning...she's facing Marlowe! Oh my God, Corta is running now! This is it! Sabrina Corta is running to meet Marlowe Kana in the center of the field!"

Sweat and dirt and blood streaked across Marlowe's face as the wind sheared down. Corta ran as fast as her injured leg permitted to confront Marlowe. Both soldiers clenched their jaws and narrowed their eyes. Exhausted, bloodied, and nearly beaten, they hurtled toward each other to end the fight and show the entire nation who was truly the superior soldier.

Suddenly, the footage on-screen wobbled. Marlowe and Corta both stopped dead in their tracks.

"What just--" Robert Roberts said before the audio to the feed was cut.

The suddenly silent footage showed Marlowe and her crew looking confusedly at the sky. Corta pointed at something just beyond the camera drone's field of vision. On-screen, her figure became blocky and pixelated. Streaks of distortion turned everyone on screen into blobs of orange and blue and purple and pink, cutting their figures into squares and rectangles. A slight crackle and a light pop sounded from the precinct's speakers before the screen went completely black.

28. The Night The Lights Went Out In Georgia

The entire waiting room of the United American State Army 12th precinct gasped in unison, then erupted in a roar of outrage, echoing the reaction of everyone else in the nation at that moment. The yellow Intercontinental Championship belt that Ama Afua had earned that morning clattered to the floor as she shot out of her chair to her feet. "What the fuck!" She yelled.

"Ama!" Her mother snapped in shock.

"Young lady!" Her father yelled. "That is…wha? What's going on?"

The lights and screens in the station flickered briefly, and then suddenly blinked off. The sound of air circulating through vents ceased. Red lights clicked on and illuminated the room with an eerie, crimson glow. Within seconds, the room grew noticeably warmer.

"Sarge?" The private asked nervously.

"Radio HQ. Find out what's going on," the sergeant responded.

"No radios, sir," the private responded.

"What's going on, officer?" Victor Smith-Afua asked.

"Yeah, and what the hell happened to MK and Corta?!?" Wallace added.

"I have no idea, and I have no idea. But I need you all to stay seated and calm," the sergeant boomed authoritatively to the room. "I'm sure this is a temporary situation, and everything is under control."

"You're *sure*?" Angela Afua asked.

"It is, ma'am," the sergeant reassured her. "Now, please just stay seated and quiet."

"Listen, officer," Angela snapped back. "I have been beaten, yelled at, taken into custody for defending my baby, and now everything is dark and it's getting hot, and you want to tell me you're *sure* everything's fine?"

"Yeah, what the hell!" Wallace yelled as he stood from his seat. "Your guns don't even work, and you got your asses kicked by Marlowe Kana earlier! How can you tell us you have anything under--"

"Sir!" the sergeant yelled as he stomped toward Wallace, "Sit down, *now*!" The soldier pulled a collapsed baton from a pouch on his belt. He whipped it forward, expanding it. Rearing back, he swung the baton at Wallace's ribs. Wallace collapsed in a gasping heap.

"Hey!" One of the other people in the waiting room of the station yelled in horror. "You can't do that!" There's rules!"

"Detail!" The sergeant ordered as he pointed at the person who had yelled. Two privates approached the man and grabbed him by the throat and around the waist. More soldiers approached from hallways and doorways, swarming in like ants from a disturbed nest.

"Secure every one of these people," the sergeant ordered.

The officers approached the citizens seated and standing in the room. Cuffs snapped across wrists. One soldier approached the Afua family.

"Don't you touch my baby!" Angela Afua snarled, wrapping her arms around her daughter.

"Ma'am, we won't hurt the girl," the officer insisted as he reached for Ama. "Please let her go and hold out your wrists--"

"You son of a bitch!" Victor Afua yelled as he swung at the officer's face, clocking him square in the jaw. Another citizen stood and grabbed the chair he had been sitting in, brandishing it in front of him like a shield. Citizens faced off against officers as the suffocating heat rose in the precinct, much as it was across the city of Atlanta.

*****

The Courtland Street Waffle House location in Atlanta held the record for most consecutive days open since the ceasefire had been declared during the Second Civil War: Fifty-one years, one hundred and twenty-four-day record. And Marc Winter was about to break it. He vigorously waved a paper Waffle House menu in front of him, trying to evaporate the sweat that rolled in beads down his face. Walking over to the door, he pulled down the metal shutters that kept it secure in the unlikely event that a Waffle House should ever have to close.

But after the third AutoCycle trash compactor machine had been yanked from the post it was anchored to outside and thrown at the windows in front of his store, Marc decided that this event, unlikely as it may have been, was worth breaking the record.

"Kids, stay down," Marc ordered as he reached for another window shutter.

Reginald and Regina Todd, and their weird friend Tad did as he ordered.

*****

"Oh my god!" Matthew Swift's father gasped as he looked out of the window of his stalled, formerly hovering limousine. "How are we going to get inside our home?"

"Well, I'm sure not going out there!" Matthew said. "In this heat, we'll die!"

Just then, a rock flew from the sidewalk across the street from them, smashing through the back window of the vehicle. The limousine began rocking back and forth on the fulcrum of the rounded maglev engine underneath.

"Dad!" Matthew yelled in terror, watching as his father was dragged through the smashed back window. His mother shrieked as the window on her side shattered, and she was yanked by her hair through the opening. The seat Matthew was sitting on became damp with his own urine as terror washed over him.

*****

Matt and Angela Tuffner walked outside into their sun-scorched front yard. The snow had melted and the streets were steaming as heatwaves radiated across the neighborhood. Immediately, they rushed back inside and closed the door, not wanting any of the comparatively cooler air to escape.

"Oh, god," Angela said desperately to Matt, "I bet the hospital is a disaster!"

"...Ang, you can't!" Matt said in equal parts fear and anger.

"It's my job!" she replied. "I have to get there!"

Matt shook his head. He didn't want his wife to go; he was terrified that she would suffer burns from the increasingly toxic, boiling air or perhaps even be killed. But he also knew that keeping Angela from helping others, especially during an emergency would absolutely be a non-option. He sighed. "We can take the bikes," Matt said.

"You're coming?" Angela asked in surprised delight.

"Well, the Playstation 12 is dead, so I've got nothing else to do…" He gave her the smile that had made her fall in love with him ten years before.

*****

Glen Russel ducked as a five-pound weight plate sailed over his head and crashed into the screen on the wall behind him.

"C'mon, man. Be reasonable!" Glen yelled.

"Screw you!" the angry gymrat hollered back. "I don't owe you those pushups, auggie!"

"You do!" Glen demanded. "Mad Dog didn't lose!" Before he could hurl the weight in his hand, he felt a cable from a shoulder-pull machine wrap around his neck and yank back tightly.

Omar Rodriguez was lying on the floor of his apartment in a pool of his own sweat. The heat was oppressive, but more so was the stench of the months of unwashed clothes in his hamper permeating the air. It was also, in fact, rivaled by the odor of the two garbage bags lying near his front door, waiting for the day he decided to actually throw them into the Autocycle bin at the end of his hall...or fix the one in his own apartment.

"I gotta get out of here," he said aloud, as if to motivate himself off the floor. He rolled to his belly and crawled to the door. Ever so slowly, he rose to his feet, finding even standing to be excruciating in the over-one-hundred-degree heat. He opened the door to his apartment.

The smell of the garbage rotting in the Autocycle machine at the end of the hall punched him in the face and he reflexively slammed his apartment door shut.

"Fucking automated super," he cursed. *Nothing ever works around here... That's what I get for staying in Imagen housing.*

*****

Brittany Millar lay sobbing in her father Brian's lap. "But I have to know!" she repeated for the fifth time.

"I'm sorry, honey," Brian Millar said to his daughter. "There's no network. No J.A.Q.i. I can't ping anyone and nothing is online."

"But I don't understand!" Brittany said. "How do we have power but no one else does?!"

"We have our own power, sweetie," David explained again to his daughter. "We're not attached to the grid--"

Just then, a knock sounded from the door. "Open up!" A loud voice boomed. "We know you got power!"

"Let us in!" Another voice yelled. "Or we'll break down the door!"

David stood and aimed at the door the antique pre-war shotgun his father had given him.

"Careful!" Brian said. "We don't even know if the ammo works!"

Brian aimed the firearm at the door.

A loud *THUD!* came from the door, followed by another. And then a third *THUD*, with a loud *CRASH*, followed by a deafening *BOOM*!

"It works," Brian said grimly to his husband as one man fell in a pool of his own blood, and two others took off running through the night.

*****

The workshop-turned-headquarters for The Sovereign was suddenly eerily silent - a stark contrast to the din that Sully and William were valiantly trying to ignore just a moment earlier. The audio and video of several dozen Feeds covering Marlowe's fight against Corta at the Terminus Citadel had suddenly ceased. The silence was spectacularly eerie. And Sully didn't like eerie.

"What the hell just happened?" Sully asked, laying down his playing cards.

"I have no idea," Austin responded from his hacker terminal. Everything just...died."

"What did you do??" Sully demanded.

"Well, I didn't do *that*!" Austin answered. "It's a complete outage! All nodes within a half mile of the Terminus Citadel are black! Pods, home nodes, relays... even drone repeaters. All dead. It's like an EMP just went off and fried everything... "

"Well if you didn't, who did?"

They both looked over at The Judge, who was leaning against William's workbench. He had his perennial smirk stamped across his face. "J.A.Q.i, raise Hank Collins," The Judge ordered through his hacked Pod.

A tone sounded in The Judge's ear and a small video screen appeared in his heads-up display.

"It's time," he ordered.

"On it now," Hank replied calmly.

"That was you?" William asked The Judge warily from across the room.

The Judge smiled wide. "It's time for us to make ourselves known," he said. "What better way than this?"

Sully and William exchanged looks. Both shrugged.

"Think this is part of his plan?" Sully whispered to William from behind his card hand.

"If it isn't, it is now," William replied. "Eights?"

"Go fish," Sully responded, as William reached out to take a card.

29. Right Here, Too Much

"No luck, sir!" Cook's aide shouted from the doorway of the Situation Room in the underground bunker of the New White House. "Everything within the Atlanta city limits is dark. I can't reach Mayor Benjamin."

"Goddammit, Marcus," Cook replied, "I don't care if someone has to fly there personally, you *find* Andre and you get him on my private line as soon as possible!"

"Yes, sir!" Marcus said as he exited the room and shut the door.

Cook turned back to Generals Baker and Heinsman, who were seated at the table in order to his left. "Where are we at?" Cook asked.

"Zero visibility," General Baker reported. "No cameras, biometrics, monitors…Fulton and Dekalb atmosphere generators are still dark."

"Do we know yet if they're truly offline or if it's just a coms interruption?"

"Undetermined, sir. They are priority one and two once reinforcements arrive."

"Where are we on that?"

"A full battalion is prepping now, sir," General Heinsman responded.

"Deploying in thirty," General Baker added.

"Make it two battalions and get them out the door in fifteen minutes."

"But, sir," General Baker responded. "That will almost certainly compromise the local operations of other cities in the nat—"

"Two battalions in Atlanta within the hour, or it's your asses!" President Cook snapped. He turned to his right, where the Director of WarFeed Broadcasting sat. "Jim, cameras?"

"I've got two hundred camera drones diverting from Chattanooga now, and another four hundred en route from Nashville and Memphis, sir," Jim replied. "I can double that number by noon."

"See?" Cook said as he looked back at the generals. "*This* is the kind of response I am looking for! Great work, Jim." His attention moved further down the table. "Candice?"

"No one has claimed responsibility for the EMP yet, sir," The Strategic Office Chief answered. "Gaslanders resurfacing is always a safe bet, but early intel suggests that it's the group who sprung Marlowe Kana yesterday."

"Issue a release to NewsFeed. Tell them it was a fault in eaOS 12.2 and we are issuing an emergency update as we speak. We can't scare the public with terror threats this time around."

"Already done, sir," the Chief replied.

"Excellent," Cook replied. Michael?"

"Literally putting the dots on the i's of your speech right now, sir," the Director of Public Relations replied.

"Has anyone reached Davis?" Cook asked.

"No, sir," Pam Daly, the newly appointed Ambassador to Imagen Corporation replied.

"Find a way," Cook said. "I already know the answer, but I have to ask again. Is there ANY response from ANY beacon, node, drone, vehicle, or person inside the Atlanta city limits?" Cook queried the room.

Silence.

"Damn," Cook said, lowering himself into his seat. "Engagement was the highest it's ever been in history..."

"The numbers were staggering, sir," General Heinsman replied. "A few hundred thousand short of every single citizen in the nation. Your engagement strategy worked, sir."

"Yes, until it didn't!" Cook snapped. "Who could have possibly…" He slammed the table in front of him with his fist and yelled "Davis!" Everyone in the room flinched.

"Generals," Cook ordered, "I want you to begin working up a strategy for a hostile takeover of the Imagen Corporation's headquarters."

General Baker and General Heinsman both gasped. "Sir…"

"Commander-In-Chief, remember?" Cook replied nastily.

"Sir, we have satellite visual coming from Atlanta," the Director of Citizen Welfare announced. "It's…it's red, sir."

"What?" Cook asked. "Like, the footage is colored red?"

"No sir," The director replied. "The entire city's power grid is down. The situation is red, sir."

Cook studied the screen. The satellite's camera was zooming in, bringing the city closer and closer into view. An overlay of the nation's power grid showed a web of red over the perimeter of Atlanta, indicating entire carrier lines were offline.

"Jesus," General Baker said. "That means--"

"--no atmospheric generators," General Heinsman answered in shock. "This is *bad*, sir."

"We can deal with that later," President Cook insisted. "I need plans for the Imagen Headquarters invasion drawn up and in front of me immediately! Alan Davis will *pay* for this!"

"Sir!" The Director of Citizen Welfare said again. "We've got a CitizenFeed with drone footage of Atlanta!"

"J.A.Q.i, main screen!" Cook ordered. A tone sounded, and the footage from a drone belonging to a user named ~StuntDronez~ appeared. Waves of heat were rising from the asphalt as the drone hovered around, showing citizens on the streets waving and fanning themselves with their tablet Pods, hats, and anything else they could find. Sweat was flying as two citizens fought with what little energy they could muster as they quibbled over an umbrella. The drone's on-screen display reported the temperature at a hundred and seventeen degrees Fahrenheit.

"My God," General Baker said, stunned.

"Sir, we need to mobilize every available medical and technical unit to Atlanta, immediately!"

"J.A.Q.i! Commandeer that drone, right now!" Cook ordered. "Get it to Terminus Citadel! I want eyes on the Next Top Soldiers, and I want it NOW! Find Marlowe Kana!"

"Sir, the first priority is the safety of the people!" The Director of Citizen Welfare said grimly.

"I'm the goddamn president and I am ordering you to get that drone to Terminus Citadel!" Cook barked. "And where are the plans for Imagen Headquarters?" Silence was Cook's only answer as the screen showed a drone buzzing past fighting and dying citizens, making its way through the city to Terminus Citadel.

"Sir..." Marcus, the President's aide, said from behind him as he peeked in from the doorway, "There's something you need to see...a new CitizenFeed that just started broadcasting—"

"Not the time for cat GIFs, Marcus!" Cook snapped.

"It's not that, it's...well, just look. J.A.Q.i, main screen."

"Approval, Mr. President?" J.A.Q.i asked.

Cook thought for a moment, sighed, then said, "Yes, J.A.Q.i. Approved."

The screen flickered, then showed a muscular man with short, graying black hair. A kaleidoscope of tattoos poured from the sleeves of his black t-shirt, which was emblazoned with a red fist logo.

"I am Hank Collins, and I am the voice of The Sovereign. You will be hearing from us," the man on the screen said, before it went black.

"Dammit, Marcus!" President Cook barked, "How many times do I have to tell you to rewind these things before you show them to me?"

Marcus gasped. "Sorry, sir," he said, "Let me start it from the beginning...there."

The man's face on the screen jumped and bobbed manically as his mouth flashed opened and closed, the scrubber on the video's timeline sliding back to the beginning. Suddenly, everything froze. Hank Collins stared directly into the lens of the camera, a scowl stamped on his face for a second, then two, then three...

"Play the damn thing!" Cook yelled.

"It's playing!" Marcus replied. "He's just...starting really slow, sir."

"Dramatic, much?" President Cook muttered.

Hank Collins took a deep breath on the screen, then began: "My name is Hank Collins, and I am the voice of The Sovereign. As many of you just saw, the unfair battle that Marlowe Kana was forced to fight was interrupted, much like how her life was interrupted when Imagen falsely imprisoned her…like how General Kana's freedom was interrupted when he was arrested for a false charge… just how like your life, and my life, and the lives of every United American State Citizen has been interrupted by imprisonment thanks to Imagen's over-corporatized society.

"Your entire life, you've been lied to. You have been told that you have choices: work and advance your family, or don't work and Imagen will take care of you. Go to school and advance yourself, or don't go to school and Imagen will take care of you. You've been given choices of which flavor of drink you want to drink, or food you want to eat, or what color you want your hair to be, or what type of clothing you want to wear. All of it made by Imagen. All of it controlled by one corporation. A corporation started by our so-called president's great-great-great grandfather. A corporation that controls our weather and our entertainment and our time, none of it truly ever free. A corporation that we now depend on to eat, to work, and to live. A corporation that tells us that great and necessary wars are going on outside of our borders to keep 'terrorists' in line and keep us safe.

"There is no war. There is only control. And we, The Sovereign, are *done* being controlled."

"Tonight, we announce ourselves. Tonight, we tell you that there is real choice coming. A choice for your future. A choice to be truly free. I am Hank Collins, and I am the voice of The Sovereign. You will be hearing from us."

The video faded to black.

The personnel in the Situation Room wasted no time scrambling into action. "Sir," General Baker said, "I have began running searches and harvesting intel on this Sovereign group. We should have preliminary intel back within—"

"—I know who it is," President Cook said flatly, staring down at the table while rubbing the graying temples of his head. "Run intel for Andrew Garfield, age fifty-nine, also probably known as The Judge. It's a stupid name, I know. You won't find anything, but try anyway."

"...Who is Andrew Garfield, sir?" General Heinsman asked.

Cook looked up and faced an expectant room full of his administration's greatest minds, all of whom had eyes locked on their President.

"Someone I used to know," Cook stated.

The deafening silence in the room was eventually interrupted by a tone ringing. "Sir," J.A.Q.i announced. "The drone has arrived at Terminus Citadel."

All eyes turned to the screen as the drone surveyed the area. The courtyard was flooded with prisoners who were tearing out of the front gates, spreading out in all directions as they fled. The facility's lights were dark and the once-electrified fencing was failing to keep the prisoners from climbing up and over. There was no sign of Marlowe or her squad.

"Sir," General Baker spoke up urgently. "There are nearly ten thousand felons with some degree of advance warfare training pouring into a city with no electricity, no weapons, and no soldiers," she said. "I *have* to insist that you--"

"--FINE," Cook rolled his eyes as he waved his hand at the General. "Send aid and tech services to Atlanta. And one of the United American State Army battalions."

"Right away, sir!" General Baker replied.

"But only the one!" Cook insisted. "The other one is headed to Indianapolis. To Imagen."

30. Materfamilias

Marlowe felt herself waking. There was no dream from which she woke, and no noise woke her. One moment she wasn't, and the next, she was. Awareness simply *happened*.

"Is she awake?" a voice that came from everywhere asked. Marlowe instinctively scanned around. She was in a kind of glass tank. She couldn't see anything. All around her was darkness. The voice was coming from a woman behind the glass.

"She is?" The voice queried. "Good. Hello, Marlowe. I'm Dr. Patel. You are in my lab. We are on Oz. You're safe."

Marlowe's eyes tried to focus through the liquid in the tank. She tried to scream. A few bubbles skirted past the tube in her throat, floating from out of her mouth and up to the surface of the tank. She tried to struggle. Her legs wouldn't cooperate. She couldn't lift her arms. She couldn't even rotate her head in any direction. The only thing in her body that responded was her heart, which began pounding violently.

"Sedation. Now," Marlowe could barely hear Dr. Patel give the order. Slowly, her panic subsided. "Judging from the sudden spike in your heart rate," the doctor's voice said once again, "I'm sure you're quite confused. Maybe even scared. There really is no need to be. Once again, I assure you, you are safe. Conserve your energy. You're in terrible shape, and there's a lot of work to do."

Marlowe felt her heart rate dropping. She couldn't feel her body, and yet she sensed tension leaving her jaw and cheeks.

"Good!" Dr. Patel said. "Now, we are going to lower the shield around the tank so you can see what's going on. The light isn't necessarily bright, but you may want to close your eyes just in case."

Marlowe refused to comply. A crack of light formed around the top of the tank and grew into a band, which widened as the shield protecting the hydrostatic tank lowered. The water distorted the objects before Marlowe, but she could just make them out — a few screens on walls, a few pieces of machinery near the tank, and a team of people in white lab coats standing behind a woman who was clearly Dr. Patel. She had a shock of white hair, with bangs that just reached the edges of her thin eyebrows. The smile lines in her face were so etched in, Marlowe could make them out from behind a thousand gallons of water in a low-lit room. The tablet-sized device she held at her waistline was almost as wide as her thin torso, and she stood several inches taller than the rest of her staff.

"There was an EMP blast at the Terminus Citadel," Dr. Patel said in lieu of formal introductions. "Your eyes, neural interface, and entire muscular system were all disabled and severely damaged. We've replaced your eyes and the interface, but your muscles…well, we've been working for six days to rebuild them and still have quite a long while to go."

Marlowe couldn't focus. A thousand questions flew through her mind like buckshot fired from a cannon, and she couldn't get her head around any of them.

The omnidirectional voice of Dr. Patel echoed through her skull once again. "You're going to be in here a while, I'm afraid," she stated. "The team discussed it and, while it wasn't unanimous, we have decided not to keep you sleeping for the duration. We have screens positioned so that you can be kept abreast of everything going on, both at home and abroad."

Marlowe could physically feel her mind strain as she tried to concentrate, this time focusing on the screens. Through the distortion of the liquid in the tank, she could see NewsFeed's Pat Daniels on a screen. There was another screen which was simply streaming a logo of a red clenched fist on a solid black background. There were other screens with logos and faces she didn't recognize, with crawls and titles in languages she couldn't read.

"Some of these Feeds will answer some of your questions," Dr. Patel said, her tone lifting up in sympathy, "but I'm sure that they'll probably leave you with far more. Don't worry, we will have plenty of time to talk once the initial phases of rebuilding your muscles are finished and you're out of the tank. In the meantime, try to relax."

Despite the sedative, Marlowe's heart rate began to rise again. She had so many questions, and the only thing worse than not having the answers to them was not being able to ask them at all. Dr. Patel watched as Marlowe's pulse quickened.

"I understand that, despite your impressive history, this must be very scary," the Doctor said reassuringly. "You are in good hands. Many of the members of this team were on the original project that created you from babyhood. They know you better than you know yourself. Well, your systems, anyway."

Marlowe's eyes widened.

"Surprised?" The doctor asked. "Surely you've wondered...you've had to have at some point. Well, let me go ahead and assuage you of any doubt — no, you are not synthetic. You're only augmented. And quite human."

Marlowe's eyes relaxed slightly over relief that her worst fear was unfounded. But immediately, her mind raced back to all of the doubts — that this team was a fraud, that she was being lied to, that this was an experiment to test her. She looked over again at Dr. Patel with worry in her eyes.

"I assure you, you're in good hands," the doctor assured her. "This team is the best in the world, and they will be working around the clock to get your body working again. I wouldn't trust just anybody with my daughter."

Marlowe's eyebrows furrowed. The first real thought formed in her mind: *Was that some kind of metaphor?*

A tone sounded on Dr. Patel's tablet. She raised it up and studied it. "No, Marlowe, it wasn't a metaphor," the doctor responded to Marlowe's unspoken question. "I am your biological mother."

Marlowe's heart rate spiked. She tried to thrash, to smash her way out of the tank and kill this monster who would dare lie to her so egregiously. A few small bubbles rose from the tube in her mouth and percolated to the top of the tank.

"Sedative!" Dr. Patel ordered. "Now!"

Marlowe's eyelids grew heavy. Her mind couldn't form words, and her thoughts slowed. Still, anger burned deep in her. She felt it glowing from the very core of her being

"We will talk, Marlowe," the doctor said, "I promise. For now, get some rest." Distantly, Marlowe heard Dr. Patel order the shield around the tank raised. Light began to diminish. The wide bar of light became narrower, until the last sliver of it slid through a crack at the top of the tank, finally disappearing, leaving Marlowe completely in the dark.

End Of Volume 3

About the Author

Joe Peacock has been writing on the internet in some form or fashion for 20 years. This is his first work of fiction, and it's scary as hell to release into the world. But he has learned a lot about writing through the process, and it has been a lot of fun working on this story. He also writes his own bios and doesn't quite know why he's doing so in the third person. He has cats and dogs and lives in Atlanta, GA.

Credits

Words and website stuff: **Joe Peacock**
Edited by: **Rowena Yow**

Cover art by **Meghan Hetrick**

Website and supporting art by **Alex Monik**

Other books by Joe Peacock

Please visit your favorite ebook retailer to discover other books by Joe Peacock:

The Marlowe Kana Series
    Volume 1
    Volume 2
    Volume 3 (This book!)
    Volume 4 (Coming soon!)

Mentally Incontinent: That Time I Burned Down a Hooters, That Time My Stalker Crashed on My Couch, and Nine Other Stories from My Weird Life

Everyone Deserves To Know What I Think: Collected Writing, 2003-2013

Follow Joe Peacock on Social Media:

Facebook: http://facebook.com/joepeacock
Twitter: http://twitter.com/joethepeacock
Blog: http://www.joepeacock.com/
Email: Joe@joepeacock.com

Follow Marlowe Kana on the web and read the next volume (and all future volumes) for FREE:

Facebook: http://facebook.com/marlowekana
Twitter: http://twitter.com/marlowekana
Tumblr: http://marlowekana.tumblr.com/
Instagram: http://instagram.com/marlowekana

Read the whole book free!
Get extra art, downloads and more:

http://www.marlowekana.com/

Made in the USA
Columbia, SC
19 November 2017